ATLANTIS

DOWNFALL OF THE MOTHERLAND

by

Michael E. Morgan

ATLANTIS

DOWNFALL OF THE MOTHERLAND

For information write to:
Dawntrader Books, LLC
P.O. Box 261
Wilton, Connecticut
06897

If you are unable to order this book from your local bookseller, or Amazon.com, you may order directly from the publisher.
Quantity discounts for organizations are available.

Edited by Sal Glynn San Francisco
Many Thanks to Alexa Lombardi for her illustrations

Cover and book design by
Michael E. Morgan

Publisher's Cataloging-in-Publication Data
ISBN 978-0990-313-380

10 9 8 7 6 5 4 3 2 1

Table of Contents

Introduction

The fable of *Atlantis, the Lost Continent*, manages to trigger fascination and wonder as would be the idea of finding a treasure trove of pirate's gold, such as, the mystery of Oak Island and the treasure of Black Beard which still haunts treasure hunters up to this day. The Atlantis fable was lost to antiquity until archeologists and philologists began to scrutinize Plato's dialogues, *'Timaeus and Criteas'* along with his discussions about the perfect democracy in the *"The Republic.'*

Plato would often test his logic and theories by way of mixing his philosophy with storytelling to Aristotle, his mentor. This fact would be responsible for shrouding the potential of the fable being considered as fragments of the truth.

Perhaps, in the same way, the fate of the city of Troy by Homer in *Ulysses*, also considered as the fanciful meanderings of literary license until the remains of Troy were actually uncovered. The city of Ur, central to the Sumer civilization also considered mythical, until recently, the ruins of Ur were found. In 1990 the Marine Archeological Society of India, discovered the lost city of Dwarka, mythical city in the Sanskrit epic

Mahabharata, also considered a mythological dissertation and would have remained so, if it weren't for a tidal wave that pulled back the waters to reveal its location.

While the ideas of Plato were debated in the halls of prestigious universities, other writers/explorers began to explore Plato's descriptions of the motherland with a great deal of interest and study. One such author was Ignatius Donnelly, in his work, '*Atlantis, The Antediluvian World.*'Perhaps Donnelly's inspiration came from a quote by Festus:

'*The world has made such comet-like advance lately on science, we may almost hope, before we die of shear decay, to learn something about our infancy, when lived that great, original, broad-eyed sunken race, whose knowledge, like the sea-sustaining rocks, hath formed the base of this world's fluctuous lore.*'

Like many new fields of endeavor arising during the 19th century renaissance, adventurous truth seekers explored, in their writings, the mysterious and wondrous myths of ancient tales.

Donnelly's writing was no different. In his case, the exception was that he took the idea of the myth to be true and tried to use the commonality of artifacts and similarity of tales from unconnected regions which all seemed to relate and point to their apparent origin, somewhere in the middle of the Atlantic Ocean.

He expanded the idea beyond the minor pandering of others to great lengths, revealing many details of the legend. No doubt, his beliefs were centered on the basic idea that all great religions, all nations and their cultures from thousands of years in the past, have their roots from the one 'motherland.'

To quote from his book:

'This book is an attempt to demonstrate several distinct and novel propositions. There once existed in the Atlantic Ocean, opposite the mouth of the Mediterranean Sea, a large island, which was the remnant of the Atlantic continent, and known to the ancient world as Atlantis. That description of this island given by Plato is not, as has been supposed, fable, but veritable history.'

In the modern age of archeology in the twenty

first century, many remarkable discoveries have occurred, such as, the underwater ruins of monolithic structures off the coast of Japan purported to be 12,000 years old. The investigations by John Anthony West regarding the true age of the Sphinx and the great pyramid of Gizeh in Egypt, not created by the ancient Egyptian culture 3500 years BC, the age considered to be the height of their culture, but far older, beyond 10,000 years ago.

These considerations come into light when the striations along the side of the sphinx have been determined to be from water levels of the Nile river far higher than now, known to be more than 10,000 years before.

The Gizeh pyramid is purported to be built by the pharaoh, Khufu, because his cartouche is labeled on the inside entrance. Yet, it is well known by Egyptologists that Pharaohs of various dynasties would claim these great artifacts as their own to enhance their god like status. Cartouches are known to be written vertically, the cartouche found by Howard Vyse in 1837, was horizontal and some suspect the archeologist drew the cartouche by himself, so he could have something to claim.

There is the discovery of remarkable ruins of Kobekli Tepe in Turkey. These artifacts exhibit features that astound even the most scenical of investigators. Their incredible engineering and precise cutting techniques suggest scientific skills far beyond the skills of common stone age cultures and builders.

On the other hand, other supernatural resources, such as, psychics and clairvoyants have reported details regarding the lost continent in their readings. One such clairvoyant in the early twentieth century, known as the Sleeping Prophet, Edgar Cayce, proposed many details of the Atlantean culture and existence during several hypnotic recalls.

While many scoff at such ridiculous proposals, the fact is, records of his readings report that a portion of Atlantis would rise again off the coast of Bimini in the Bahamas in 1930. An Atlantean road, then underwater, would be rediscovered in the Bahamas in the early 60s, decades later after his death. Jacque Cousteau's diving team discovered such a road off the coast of Bimini, a large monolithic stone road exposed after a storm removed tons of ocean silt obscuring them from view, leading outward toward the ocean.

Now, many private groups have taken up the search for evidence of the lost continent. One such archeological dig is on the isle of Santorini. Following the concept that the island sank in one day and one night, the belief that the caldera of Santorini reduced a culture to ruins nearby, engulfing it in a huge volcanic and subsequent tidal flood. Though this may be true, the location of this catastrophic event doesn't match the location of Plato's descriptions. The culture lost to that volcanic disaster was actually Minoan, not Atlantean, as noted by some scholars.

Since the myth describes an apocalyptic flood causing the demise of the island, the timing agrees with the legend, occurring some 12,500 years BC. A flood account that rests with both scriptural and other legends from many cultures throughout the world, suggest the possibility the earth experienced a major pole shift where continents moved around. This idea, of a 35-45-degree shift in the poles, would offer a plausible argument.

This idea, though challenged by the scientific community, suggests perhaps that where they are looking is totally wrong. Perhaps they should be looking at other possible locations relating to the new land masses, such the Azores, or perhaps south, toward Antarctica. Interestingly, recent activity in the region of Antarctica has become top-secret. No one can go there without clearance. There are many conspiracies surrounding this ice covered continent.

The famous Piri Reis map dated 1513, shows incredible details of the Antarctica coast line now under miles of ice. It would indicate that Antarctica was free of ice at one time. Those coastal details were recently confirmed by satellite X-ray photography. It may indicate the Reis map is a copy of a much older document but there is no further evidence to prove that.

Even Admiral Byrd reported to the Military Joint Chiefs in 1947, after his command of a deployment of military forces under the code name, 'Operation High Jump', a secret mission to remove purported Nazi encampments in Antarctica after the war.

At the end of World War 2, the United States conducted a survey of German Uboats and found more than 150 Uboats missing from the tally. It was rumored that the German High Command took those Uboats, engineers and scientists along with supplies and advanced technology in 1939, first to Argentina then south to Antarctica, where it was believed an advanced rear-guard base was developed even before the Germans attacked Poland. They called this rear-guard base Neuswabenland.

The raid by Admiral Byrd was quickly crushed by strange unknown craft emerging from the ice. These craft, he described with some alarm. He said these craft outmaneuvered his planes and successfully destroyed many ships and aircraft and killing thousands of troops. The craft could fly from pole to pole in a matter of hours. The task force was gutted and they retreated with only a small remainder of their forces. Byrd was debriefed for 5 days by the military and given a gag order not to speak to the press for many years.

I lived in a boarding house, while working at a publishing company and attending some college courses since leaving high school. One of three living in the house was a strange man, who lived alone, but enjoyed exploring all over the world. He was an avid studier of the civil war. His room was close to hoarder status, as he had hundreds of books he collected and stacked in several columns throughout his living room. It was so tight that walking through his living room was more like entering and negotiating a cave with a maze.

He was a member of the Pan American Clipper club, with that airline then still running at the time. He had gone to Africa and discovered an unknown water fall in the Congo region, named it after his girlfriend. After a year, he received an invitation from the National Geographical Society of Explorers to attend a dinner party given in honor of Admiral Byrd.

I asked him if he got the chance to talk with him personally, to ask about 'Operation High Jump' and the polar opening of the earth at the North pole. My friend was dubious about my request since he had no knowledge of Byrd's exploits in that way. When he returned, I was delighted to hear that Byrd confirmed these aspects of his exploits.

Perhaps, the legend of Atlantis will remain an unsolved mystery, left to future generations to uncover it's location and the remains of proposed advanced technology enjoyed so long ago.

Perhaps, the United States has already discovered the remnants of this lost civilization under the ice in Anarctica, hence why a top-secret clearance is needed to go there now.

Recently, top US political officials have visited the southern continent under the guise of secret mission investigations.

The history of the world, the world of Atlantis is complex, covering a tale of epic proportions spanning a period of hundreds of thousands of years. A prediluvian period of prehistory long before the earliest paleolithic stone age began.

The story from Solon, the law giver, in the land known later as Greece, given to a philosopher called Plato it is said, came from the earlier archives of another land, in the once famous library of Alexandria, Egypt. The story he told was incomplete, however. It described a little of my culture in its last stages before the final deluge and destruction. It was a story of the last surviving island, which existed 11,200 years before what you would call the common era.

Originally, our great continent sat in the middle of the large body of waters surrounding the continent, now called the Atlantic. It stretched to what is now called Bimini to the south and the Azores to the north. It existed beyond the Pillars of Hercules (the 'rock of Gibraltar', the only remaining half of that marker after the great changes occurred and the time of ice came), beyond what is now known as the Mediterranean

Sea. The island was the last of five islands that originally made up the continent after our first catastrophe.

In those days, there were two orbs encircling the earth, our names for them were Liloth and Raika. Two lands covered the planet, our continent to the east and Gwandana to the west, comprising a region of the land our people called Mu.

The keeper of records described the emergence of our ancestors arising from the sea. As sea creatures, they emerged from the waters one day and walked onto the land. In those days, the land was filled with all manner of monsters.

Unlike the warm waters of the sea, holding a constant temperature from undersea volcanic eruptions, the surface of the lands was wildly different and constantly changing. Our ancestors developed thick fur for protection and made their dwelling places high in the trees far above and away from the monsters roaming the land.

Later, the ancestors divided into two tribes. The first tribe refused to stay on the cold dangerous land and slipped back into the waters again, retreating to where the waters and land joined. The land we called Mu was the land of waters.

Later, the land-tree ancestors were told by the gods it would be better to descend from the trees and forage for food, while seeking refuge from the monsters in caves. The record keepers told us that our wisdom originated hundreds-of-thousands of cycles of the One, the light giver, which became our chief god, the One Most High, maker of the Law of One.

Our tribe honored the One by building many temples in our land to protect us from the monsters. The temples were adorned with replicas of our ancestoral mascots, those whom you call dolphins now, as well as, the first Law Givers.

Our culture began to grow slowly. As we gathered together, growing in numbers believing, as we were assured, many gathered together would provide greater safety.

The continent, comprised of several different landscapes, which helped to form what would become later, as the 6 great clans. The highlands were defined by three mountains to the north; Scartera a volcanic mountain, and its sister Palinor and brother, Sepula. While the low lands to the south, defined by a great valley, we called the Valley of the Wind. It enjoyed a constant warm wind blowing from the inlet sea. That inlet would become our harbor later, the main entrance to the City of the Realm.

While our culture continued to grow and develop, it was clear that various traits and skills needed to be organized. In our culture, energy and the gathering of it was supreme. We were very taken by ways to maximize our effective productivity to the whole of the colony. The colony became more like a hive community.

We developed along the lines of what would become known as the Natural Forces of nature. Those Natural Forces were symbolized by two great dragons, an Earth Dragon and the Sky Dragon. The wisdom of our ancestors and the gods, defined the consciousness of our environment and the importance of being harmonious with the dragon energy, which became the underpinning of our philosophy of life.

Eventually, the clans sought greater organization with leaders providing direction and purpose. Each tribe or clan, defined by their locale and skills; The Baal Clan-the makers; The Yaga Clan-the builders; the Faeylan Clan-hunters and fishermen; the Saliene clan-farmers; the Tasher clan-the priesthood and gazers; The Togal clan-warriors. Each clan had a representative reflecting the various needs of the clan. Soon the various needs of the clans needed to be combined, so a High Council of clans came into being.

The Council functioned by way of what you would call a democratic process, whereby, each Council member had a vote. At times, the votes became deadlocked and would not progress forward with a measure of productive success. It was agreed by all, that one would be chosen as a Supreme Leader, or king, for the sole purpose of making sure there would be a majority to go forward.

Reproductive activities were governed by the Tasher clan. They were those who observed the heavens and the ways of the lights in the sky, in particular, the One and the two orbs that encircled the planet. The gazers realized the movements between the One and the orbs controlled the growth of crops. Weather patterns could also be determined in advance.

Then it was clear, that the path of life in Atlantis should also be governed by those lights. Thus, reproduction was controlled and determined not by emotional desires or needs, but by the stars above.

Because the stars were responsible for the outpouring of offspring, ownership of offspring became a common chattel of the colony, until coming of age, the children were kept in hatcheries, their existence became the responsibility of everyone.

Energies were understood to emerge from two great dragons, the Earth Dragon and the Sky Dragon. Their enter-twining defined the way. Our way of life flowed with the balance of these forces of heaven and earth.

The ones gifted with insight were originally given the task to ensure that the Sky Dragon and the Earth Dragon would not be violated and remain in balance. These were the priests of the Temple of the Law of One, those of the Tasher clan.

The protectors of the realm came from the highlands, they being of the mountains, possessed the awesome power of the three mountains and so, were the strongest, they were the Tec warriors of the Togal clan, warriors sworn to defend the Realm.

Those that seemed inclined to understand the way of mechanical things were the Baal clan, they were the makers of things. Those that were responsible for the growth and harvest of the food supply were the Saliene Clan, in honor of the God Saliene, of agriculture and abundance.

My story begins with my youth. I am Raag, Prince Regent of the Realm, first in line of succession to the royal line of King Tatsukin, along-side is my sister, Itala, my confidant and best friend. We reside in the great City of the Realm, within the walls of Falcanah, the Citadel of the King.

I have been selected by the overseers, the members of the High Council and my father, to lead the hunt for the Beshinwar, a great and powerful beast that traditionally provides the main course for the feast of Mahadi. This is the festival of the two orbs encircling the planet.

To hunt the Beshinwar is to honor the gods of fertility, and agricultural abundance. Moreover, its

timely slaughter, at the conjunction of the two
orbs, is important to the welfare of the Realm, as
its sacrifice is to the god Ishtar, giver of light and
life, the One Most High.

It is a great honor bestowed upon me, though I
must admit, I am inexperienced with this task. I
must gather my courage and cunning. The task also
becomes a test of my courage, strength and
wisdom to lead the Realm, as my father's
successor. It is a test that I must not fail.

I am filled with concern about my ability to
carry out this formidable task. I will be leading a
party of experienced hunters, those skilled with the
long lance, others skilled with the bow and a Tec
warrior skilled with the sword. No doubt they will
be dubious of my lack of leadership experience.
And so, the story begins.

The light of the One(sun) crested upon the highest peak of Scartera, which meant it would be dark soon. Scartera, a volcanic mountain situated in the western highlands of the continent, would often erupt unexpectedly. The caldera thrust clouds of ash high into the sky, casting reddish hues and posed ominous threats to the village below. The warm glow of orange light danced along the cracks and crevices of the mountain's shear rock face providing greater definition to its towering height.

The darkness would bring certain danger for the hunting party in search of the Beshinwar, a wingless ten-foot-tall reptile-bird. Its long upright tail and muscular legs enabled the creature very sudden and swift movement.

Though it would quickly retreat from almost any perceived danger, if cornered, became quite ferocious using its tail to bash. Its three-toed upper legs bore large claws used to protect its upper thorax and would grapple limbs of the Jub Jub tree for its fruit. The long-hooked beak set between its small hazel colored eyes hid razor-sharp teeth buried inside, capable of tearing at the unprotected flesh of an approaching hunter.

At times, they seemed incredibly resilient to capture, often requiring more than 5 hunters in a party. All hunters believed the Beshinwar to be protected and beloved by Saliene, the God of courage and abundance. Further, to kill a Beshinwar, bestowed the spoils of courage to its victors.

As the last rays of light dropped below the horizon, dependency on sight gave way to smell. In the lower ground, the air hung thick and wet. The plush undergrowth, contrasted against slender Popul palms and Soab trees all with the buzzing sound of huge insects scratching and eating.

The hunting party scouted for three days without one sighting of their prey. The team leader Raag, regent prince of the realm, decided to lead the party to higher ground.

A solemn mood lingered amongst the members of the party. They grew weary of the higher climb, worried about entering the uncharted regions above. Visions of returning home with the great beast's carcass draped over their rack, carried proudly over their shoulders, faded quickly. With the onslaught of night, uncertainty and tension grew stronger.

When they entered a small clearing within the forest below the tree line, fears of their survival weighed heavily along with concerns over Raag's lack of experience further burdened their difficult trek. Despite complaints from the others, Raag felt confident of his decision to take the higher ground. During their climb, he felt a strong sense of pride reaching up to fill his heart from the valley below. The vestiges of comfort and solace, born of his royal position now far and away did little to support. Secretly, he wished for the experience like the others, to fill that hollow void taunting him.

The time of Mahadi soon approaches, a five-day festival when the two moons, Raika and Liloth became conjunct. During the festival, all of the people from all of the clans migrated to the Valley of the Wind. They would drink the fermented juice of the Scawberry, feast on the roots of the Soab and most importantly, the tender meat of the roasted Beshinwar. Afterward, they would exchange their discoveries, experiences and newly developed skills through the sacred dance of Mahadi. In addition, the all-important public declaration by the king confirming the next succession to the throne, Raag prince regent.

The High Council of the realm bestowed upon Raag and the hunting party the honor and noble deed, to hunt and bring the meat of the Beshinwar for the celebration feast. Even though Raag was considerably younger than the rest of the party, He was chosen by the regional elder-governors to lead the hunt as his initiation to become Aire elect.

The air became thin and noticeably dry. Raag's nostrils expanded and heaved to the smell of a pungent odor. The odor drifted in front of the Tec warrior walking on point ahead of the party. The odor caused the warrior to stop abruptly.

Tec warriors belong to the Togal Clan of the high country. They are known for their fierceness and brutal courage in the face of mortal danger. They are reluctant nor moved to express strong feeling easily. The strongest of all tribes, they are trained to mold the shape of their feelings into weapons they can trust as allies. This Tec warrior bore the name of Gan, the Upanis-han, a legend, known as a mighty river to his clan, Togal.

The Tec's stillness suggested caution. This

action moved through the party like a bolt of white fire thrown down by the Thunder God Tyree.

Gan Stared intently to the left side of their path towards a small ravine. Raag broke his stride to move closer to Gan, as a show of strength and alliance. The others huddled nearby to wait for some encouragement.

For a moment, Raag's anger flared, frustrated by the delay and his lack of performance. The rising emotions moved him beyond containment. Despite the potential danger he wanted to move on, but he hesitated. A challenge might cause a breach with the Tec and he needed Gan's experience as a strong ally.

He stared silently at Gan, hiding his anger with a smile that revealed some of his crooked teeth. He watched as a single bead of sweat trickled into Gan's right eye. This did not break his concentration. Gan's ability to resist the burning salt momentarily derailed Raag's feeling. He could not hide his shape from Gan. Gan broke his gaze upon the ravine long enough to acknowledge the inner struggle within Raag to hold back the intense feelings.

Gan began.

"You are not a Tec, Raag, son of King Tatsukin. You would do well to hold true to your own shape. Your feelings betray you."

Raag returned.

"So, what captures the interest of Gan and delays our progress?"

Gan replied sharply.

"I smell the decay of flesh nearby. It is a familiar odor to me and calls forth memories of battle. My alertness is aroused to the quick!"

Raag sensed the tension in the others and stood down from his challenge.

"Hold true to your purpose then Tec. Seek out this omen and perhaps it will provide fresh sign of the Beshinwar."

Raag turned to the others and gestured to rest in the forest glen out of clear view while he watched the Tec warrior negotiate the rocks at the ravine's entrance.

He was acutely aware that Gan's fierceness and courage was only superseded by his knowledge of battle.

In a true fight, he was no match for Gan. The

sting of Gan's keen estimation of him lingered. Thoughts of the Tec warrior faded to the sounds of the hunting party settling down into the forest rocks. While he observed Mornac, he felt a mixture of contempt and relish. He watched carefully as the long-lance man removed the food pouch from his arm sling, unwrapping the bindings from the soft bark of the Soab roots. The air instantly filled with the sweet smell of their juices.

Raag grew irritated by Mornac's glutinous manner. Mornac's nostrils twitched to the odor of Raag's contempt. Raag was hungry. He had to swallow his salivating juices before he could speak.

"It is barely the passing of the Eye of the One and you are ready to gorge your face again Mornac?"

Mornac ignored this remark and continued to shift his lower jaw to accommodate some drooping bark hanging to one side of his mouth. Then he purposefully smacked his lips with delight as he lopped the remaining morsel down his throat. Mornac stared at Raag while he tore another chunk apart from the tuberous stalk, pausing only to acknowledge Raags comments.

"My body growls and the climb has been difficult." He retorted proudly nodding to the others for confirmation. After all, he continued through his loud chewing…I'm a plains hunter, the highlands are unfamiliar to me. It is not my shape to seek the high ground!"

Raag countered curtly.

"It was also not my choosing that you are here now Mornac! Were it not for your excellent skill with the long-lance, I'm confident, as a member of the Baal Clan, you would not be with us on this hunt. In fact, I'm quite sure there had been some influence from the High Council."

Mornac glared. "Raag…he began…I feel your ravenous gaze and you cannot hide your weakness from my view. If you were not so stiff with royal blood and the zeal of leading this hunt, you would be nearer to me sharing this Soab root! I also suspect there was some influence with the High Council on your behalf as well, young and inexperienced prince!"

Raag retorted.

"Your vision is solid with me lance man, but I

tell you, I fear for the scent of that bark. It will surely compromise our position."

Mornac grunted with reluctant agreement to the logic of his statement. He took one more bite from the Soab stalk with a final gesture of defiance before returning the remainder of the stalks to his pouch and sling.

Gan had been gone a long time and there was no sign of his return. Raag added a harsh tone to his voice as he commanded Mornac to take the watch over the camp, while he investigated Gan's absence. Mornac nodded with approval as Raag began to trace Gan's path into the ravine. The smell that caught the trained nostrils of the Tec grew more potent, overwhelming Raag's senses.

As the stench became more fowl with each step, he thought…*It must be very near*. The sour pungence filled his lungs and brought his heart into a near beating frenzy. Raag mounted a small rock face, placing his foot on an outcropping, the sound of twigs then broke nearby and seized his breath.

Raag hunkered against the damp rock face as though it was a shroud. He was glad that his comrades could not see him hiding. The pressure against his chest was explosive. He knew he would eventually give over to the need to take a breath.

He pulled his body closer to the rock imagining he might see through the rock. Despite his prayers to the Lawgiver, the rock face did not yield its opaqueness. Then he challenged his lack of courage at once, to raise his head for a better view. The sweat rolled down his furrowed brow and into his eyes. Unlike the Tec, he wiped it away quickly.

Adrenaline flowed through his limbs while he trembled uncontrollably. Suddenly, he thrust himself above the rock with eyes widening. He found gan stooped over the carcass of a huge Jag, a large cat with giant twin fangs protruding from its gaping mouth. He stared at Gan pensively. Gan methodically probed over the cat's remains. The sight was staggering, the body strewn about randomly revealing the chest cavity gutted, as though it exploded.

Raag's eyes dropped to meet the wide-eyed glare of the great feline. He pondered about the last sight perceived by those glassy eyes. Its yawning mouth and huge white teeth frozen in a sardonic grin indicated the beast died instantly.

Then a terrible sound emerged from the dense foliage behind them. A terrifying roar deafened the ears causing the eyes to close instinctively. The ground shook violently beneath their feet.

Raag's legs suddenly felt weak. Then, another horrible sound merged with the terrible nightmare that was upon them. Raag recognized Mornac's voice hollering an outcry of great pain. His voice echoed through the canyon below in a blistering wail, leaving no doubt about Mornac's fate.

Mornac's head and shoulders slipped easily away from his body like a branch torn from the trunk of a tree. Some of his blood splattered amongst the broad green leaves of the Popul trees above, allowing the branches to shed the spilled blood like rain upon the pale moss-covered rocks below. Still clutched in the Trok's snapping teeth,(a Trok was an Atlantean term for a Tyrannosaurus Rex) was Mornac's writhing torso.

Raag sat on the rock frozen in wild-eyed horror. All of the grand and glorious moments he dreamt of ended here at the edge of the clearing. The honor of victory fell silent as the red rain descended to the forest floor. Shock moved in on him like a great numbing fog. Darkness closed in dimming his vision. He was passing out. Through the engulfing blackness, Gan's voice screamed.

"Raag… Raag, run boy! Save yourself! Gan shook his body violently as he continued to implore…You must go now my friend, he urged with a firm tug on Raag's arm…There is not a moment to lose!"

Raag protested. He mumbled…*I am dishonored…I have cost the lives of the party…I failed in my leadership to my tribe*, but Gan remained firm with his resolve.

Gan went on…

"Raag, it is my shape to preserve and protect the party, especially to you my prince. I only ask that you remember me to the High Council with honor and dignity. Now go young prince, while I still have the advantage of protecting your backside!"

Raag began to back away as the Tec warrior turned to face his inevitable fate. He looked up to see the monster grimly displaying a sharp-toothed grimace, as if to pause and consider his next prey. Raag leapt toward the lower slopes of the ravine in hopes to find a wedge of stone that could fend off violent death and dismemberment. His feet seemed to have wings. He glanced from one outcropping to another, finding surprising agility with his limbs. He swung from branch to vine and back to rock again. Yet, with his entire new-found prowess, the great bellowing beast was all but nipping at his heals.

Raag could feel the hot breath mixed with the stench of rotting flesh surrounding him. The sound of branches being crushed under the thunderous weight of the beast growing ever closer.

In a final desperate leap to escape the jaws of certain death, Raag sought the dubious safety of a small tree branch jutting from the rising face of the ravine's cliff.

The Trok, hot in pursuit, made a swiping lunge for its last tidbit of human flesh only to loosen the ground and rocks where the small tree had its footing. The tree suddenly gave way, causing the tree and Raag to plunge to the undergrowth far below. The last shades of consciousness lingered long enough to see the beast bellowing its cry of discontent echoing into the canyon while it snapped at the air above him.

The warm winds swept along the valley toward the Citadel. My father, King Tatsukin, stood on the veranda overlooking the City of the Realm. Holding a cup of fermented scawberry, he turned as I approached. We didn't talk much since the hunt. I felt guilty for all the men lost in the party.

The king said.

"It was my fault that I put you in harm's way. It was not your shape yet to lead the hunt. I wanted to provide the opportunity for you to prove yourself as a man among men. Not everyone favored your position as leader of the hunt. I used my influence and insisted."

Raag replied.

"Father, I agreed to do it because I wanted to make you proud of me. Instead I shamed the house of Tatsukin. Not only did I ruin my chances to become your successor, but I brought doubt on this house and your rulership. For that I am truly sorry. Now, the High Council blames you for the loss of the sacrificial feast and call you the bringer of bad omens for all the Clans. They are saying the goddess Ishtar is angry and wants to punish the people and withdraw her gift of abundance."

The King replied.

"Humph…he grunted…those old men are half out of their minds most of the time…I blamed it on their staring at the stars too long…They don't know what they are talking about! …Don't you concern yourself with that bunch, I'll handle them. Someday…you will have to deal with their ramblings too, but not today…I am grateful that you survived!"

Then he commanded the servants of the Citadel to bring forth his hunting bow and quiver. He loved to go hunting for Cahwyll (a form of Pterodactyl). These creatures were a great sport for the royals. Their bite could be very painful, if not deadly. That minor danger excited my father. Offering the thrill of danger made the hunt all the more attractive.

The Cahwyll, were known to nest in the Popul trees, located north of the valley of the wind, not far from the foothills of Sepula. The journey was long and several Quanah's (an Atlantean horse) would be required.

The skill to control a Quanah let alone take one on a hunt could be very difficult for many. The Tec always used them for going into battle. They were formidable looking herbivores, but very gentle. They loved to forage on the leaves of Popul trees, so this journey would please them. My father also enjoyed a deep mental and emotional connection to the beasts. He was quite young when he learned to ride them. 4 Quanahs were required for the journey. One for the king, two for his closest aids and one for the Tec who came along for security.

Galmutin, the Regent Advisor to the King, often disagreed with some of the King's decisions. In particular, he was against detente with the leadership of Mu.

Mu was the Atlantean description of the Lemurian colony on the continent of Gwandana, to the west. The Lemurians of Mu contrasted the Atlanteans in the way of fundamental physical differences. The Atlanteans were large in stature, quite muscular, bold and aggressive creatures. Whereas, the Lemurian stature was nearly half the same height. Their limbs petite and the musculature flaccid. They were not bold and aggressive, but devious and cunning. The people of Mu used their mental acuity and the capacity to create hallucinations as their main line of defense. My father used to tell me; 'Never trust a Lemurian, you must sever their bulbous head from their scrawny body before they can deceive you with their mental wiles.'

Perhaps it is possible, that Galmutin was part Lemurian, at least with his cunning. As Prince Regent of the Realm, I often had to kneel to his authority, both as an elder council member and as my father's Royal Council. I never liked or trusted him much.

The King's behavior was often complex. In one moment, soft hearted and genuinely kind and generous. Yet, he could turn to be quite tough and rude if agitated. He ruled with a strong enough hand, but the softer side emerged in his later years and was decidedly less aggressive.

The other members of the council grew less patient with this manner and held back their contempt out of respect for his age. With that thought, I forgot to mention the average life span in Atlantis was 1500 years, or revolutions of the One. Someone aspiring to a council position would not be considered ready for leadership until the age of 600 revolutions of the One, not to exclude having substantial battle experience as well. On those occasions, when I was allowed to attend council meetings, the underbelly feeling bore a distinctively negative shape toward my father.

When the King left the Citadel with his hunting entourage, Galmutin seemed strangely agitated and impatient. I dismissed my feelings but later wondered if he was up to some dark scheme.

Galmutin told the Tec soldiers guarding the Citadel gate, he would need to leave the Citadel for a time and would return the following day. Galmutin often attended to the King's affairs in a private way, free to come and go as he liked without question. This time however, he quickly made his way to the inlet sea where he had a skiff waiting to take him to a rendezvous point with a contingent of Lemurian assassins.

The assassins would ambush the king's entourage, Trapping and killing the King and his party along the way. They dared not outwardly attack, for fear of an uprising or worse, an all-out war might ensue. Their alternative plan was to sneak into their camp and poison their food supply before they returned.

Galmutin returned to the Citadel long before the King returned, giving him a perfect alibi in the matter later.

The journey was arduous and long. Though the party left early at the rising of the One, it was almost dark when they arrived at the site of the nest. These creatures would sleep after dark, hanging upside down from the limbs of the trees. At first light, they would begin to drop from the trees for their first meal. The plan at dawn's first light, bows would be loaded and their arrows launched as they first awakened, catching them off guard. The hunting team expected many to be within the nest. Practically, they expected to take down only a few before they all escaped.

The dawn emerged slowly. The King and the other archers held ready with bows strung and arrows loaded, while the Tec warrior stood by to protect the king with his sword should anything go wrong. Unfortunately, the hunting party did not expect another flock of Cahwyll streaming into the nest in a surprise early morning assault.

Within moments, there were hundreds of

Cahwyll flying into and around the nest with their own massive assault underway, the scene became pure mayhem. Now the plan switched. The move from an offensive position to a defensive position was immediate. Some of the Cahwyll broke off from their pursuit of the nest and began to attack their challengers, the hunting party. The Cahwyll dove straight into the party making it difficult to accurately hit their targets. The Tec warrior stood by the King defending him with his sword, lopping the bodies of Cahwyll in half on every approach.

The King yelled.

"Kill some of the damn things!" I do not want to return empty handed!"

One archer's bow was grabbed while another Cahwyll took his arm off at the elbow. The King's Quanah lost an ear in the battle. Before the Tec warrior had a chance to block the Cahwyll, it suddenly turned abruptly biting the King on the shoulder just as the Tec sliced the creature's head from its body.

The full light of the One shown down on the carnage below, as the King lay on the ground wounded. Suddenly, the battle seemed to subside as quickly as it began. The party mounted their Quanahs with the King barely managing to stay aloft. Now the journey home would be slower and more difficult.

Evening fell on the Citadel as the weary troop approached the main gate of the City of the Realm. The Tec called out.

"Open the gate, the King has been wounded!"

The troop entered the main courtyard and began to assist the king off his mount.

Galmutin rushed to the veranda above, thinking with some silent delight, his plan had been successful. Then he realized, Nature had usurped his devious plan with superb finesse. He had to hide his grin, knowing full well the King was doomed. It would be only hours before he suffered a painful death from the poisonous bite of a Cahwyll.

King Tatsukin died of Cahwyll poisoning two days after the hunt. The sudden loss of the monarch brought the Council into complete panic. The High Council did not wait for the burial. With the procession of his burial in progress, they met to determine who would be the successor. I was so distraught, I escaped to the Isle of Tiber, a place known to possess relaxing waters to enhance health and longevity. I wanted to forget about my shame and dishonor, to forget my right to ascend to the throne by way of descendance. They would never accept me as their Regent, not now or ever.

Galmutin's plan was not complete. There was a chance that some on the Council would still prefer the rightful aire to the throne be a descendant. So once again he plotted against the throne, my undoing. He sent Lemurian assassins to the island where I was sulking in my sorrow.

I entered a cove of warm waters and began to swim. The swimming would help to clear my head, now aching from too much fermented scawberry. Suddenly, long spindly fingers wrapped around my shoulders and across my face as I was dragged under, holding me down until I would drown.

It was a perfect plan. Later, after completing their dark deed, they would simply declare, 'Raag became so despondent from the loss of his father, he drunk too much fermented scawberry juice, slipped unconsciously into the water and drowned, so sad!' To my luck, thank the gods, a few mermen swimming nearby saw my distress from the would be Lemurian assassins. They came to my aid by attacking from behind, snapping their necks and releasing me from their hold. I motioned a greeting of gratitude toward them and they placed their webbed hand across their gilled chest to acknowledge and went on their way.

Mermen were scarcely seen anywhere around the continent. We believed them to be another mammal of the sea, mildly intelligent and treated more like a pet of the sea than an equal. Because they always treated us with gentle kindness, we always avoided killing any of them. Like the dolphins, it was forbidden to seek them out for the purposes of eating a meal.

When I returned to the City of the Realm, chaos and concern for the welfare of the colony remained high. The Council remained in deadlock once again and unable to decide. My welcome home was mixed with gladness from some and anger from others. Those who despised me, challenging my willingness to run away leaving the kingdom in disarray. To them, it was merely a continuation of my cowardness and inability to take command of the throne. Entering the Citadel from the rear, I avoided confrontation. It gave me a chance to think things through and develop a plan to take the throne by force if necessary. Then an euphony struck me. I would claim my right to rule the ancient way…by right of battle.

To suggest a rite of ascension by right of battle, I would need to choose an opponent who I knew could stand equally against me. Since I was still young and not fully developed physically, it had to be someone of equal strength, one way or the other, it would have to be a Lemurian!

I brought this before the council. They argued the idea before me, but ultimately, the Council determined it would have political advantages for the Realm if I actually won the battle. Perhaps, they concluded, would also make a decided argument for future negotiations with Mu. The battle plan was set, but I still needed to go to the Lemurian Delegation and argue for a combatant from their tribes.

A large skiff designed to sail the waters to Gwandana sat waiting at the inlet sea, docked and loaded with provisions for the journey. Two translators and two Tec warriors were assigned to escort me to the Lemurian colony. In effect, it could be treacherous to enter into an enemy stronghold. Though tensions would be high, we were not at war yet. Having Tec warriors at my side was more than comforting, lest I be taken prisoner and used as chattel for their bargaining advantage.

I smiled at the irony of that idea. The Lemurians had no idea how much disdain the High Council held for me. Using me as a negotiation advantage would have little influence on the High Council's arbitration.

Two days of sailing with prevailing winds, soon brought us within view of the Lemurian port of Sang Galan. A reception committee stood on the rock faced pier waiting for us to dock. I did not speak the Lemurian language, having only the knowledge of a few words. Even with such few words unable to pronounce those words adequately, made the addition of translators an absolute necessity.

Coming into the village, their living quarters were adjacent to pools of steaming water. Their living quarters were as mud huts that resembled small domed caves. Not accustomed to seeing many Lemurians in quantities, it was like walking through a gaggle of frog-like creatures. Their skin a lime green with splotches of yellow, smooth and wet like a salamander. Their odorous fumes exuding from their bodies revolted my senses. I had to hold my shape not to reveal my repugnance.

The supreme leader of the Lemurian clan, Ligi Sumutu, a Cephalopod, emerged from a larger hut centrally located in the village. He had two soldiers to the left and right of him with 4 others in tow. He slithered with a septer of knurled wood cupping a large pink colored crystal on top. He raised his septer above his large cranium sack holding it horizontally and cried out words I did not understand. Then all of the others sounded off behind him with what seemed to be a high-pitched scream of adulation.

I told the translators what I wanted; their best soldier to come with us to fight a battle, a dual between myself and their warrior, in the arena of the Central Square of the City of the Realm in Atlantis. Ligi turned and said something with a smile that resembled a grimace, and out of his hut came a slightly larger specimen of their kind, carrying a range of weapons hung loosely around his lower trunk. The warrior reached with his three fingers and opposing fourth finger to adjust another sling over his shoulder. Then said something to the supreme leader and he nodded.

They all stood silent while my first translator spoke.

"Prince Raag, they've accepted your challenge to a fight within the City Walls of Atlantis. They have added one extra demand in exchange."

Raag replied.

"Well what is it?"

The first translator said.

"They claim the right to keep and carry your dead carcass back to Mu for a celebration."

Raag laughed.

"Really! Well, I think they are overly confident of their victory. All right, I agree on one condition…that I get to keep their warrior's body in Atlantis for our celebration!"

After the first translator spoke my words in Lemurian, the supreme leader looked at me, then at his best warrior and smiled, I think. While the leader Ligi Sumutu returned to his hut with his entourage, the warrior looked at me and mumbled something else, which again I did not understand. Then he pointed in the direction of our skiff, so I interpreted his words to mean let's go to your water craft.

We placed the warrior in the rear compartment with a Tec warrior to stand guard. The journey to return was a bit harsh when a squall erupted in mid-transit.

The skiff tossed and rocked wildly but did not capsize fortunately. We arrived at the inlet sea port and disembarked with the Lemurian warrior displaying himself proudly to the on-looking crowds in the street.

The battle would begin at the first break of light of the One. The Lemurian entered the arena with only a broad shaped short axe and I entered with a shield and my father's sword.

The Lemurian made a swift lung at me which I attempted to block with my sword but he wasn't there! I thought…*he could not be that fast*…In that moment, I felt a sharp pain in the back of my head as I hit the ground. I spun around but saw nothing and suddenly my right leg began to bleed and the pain forced me to drop to one knee. My father's words returned to me…*Cleave the head from a Lemurian before he deceives you…* without finding my opponent I swung my sword in a circle and caught the arm of my opponent. Blood spattered on the ground for a moment but then disappeared.

Jumping to my feet, I felt his presence very close. Then using my sense of smell and my ears gave me a brief glimpse, a momentary release from the Lemurian's spellbind he held against my mind.

Anticipating his movement and calculating where he was moving to, I spun around in a return movement allowing my sword to follow evenly at the approximate height of his shoulders. Then my sword stopped suddenly. Again, blood appeared on the ground next to my feet.

Stepping back, expecting another blow from his axe, but nothing followed. Holding my sword steady for his next assault, I focused only on the pain from my leg, while following the sound of dirt shuffling nearby. Swinging again and again until I felt the sword pause for a moment. The blade met its mark. The Lemurian appeared only a few feet in front of me, falling to his knees, bleeding from the throat. Now in plain sight, I completed the act of severing his head from his body.

The council members standing along the upper rim of the arena began to clap rhythmically to celebrate my success. Galmutin appeared briefly, looking very disappointed. Then he walked away in utter disgust.

Attendants dragged the remains of the Lemurian away while many others gathered around to congratulate my victory.

Then a council member said.

"Well done young prince of the Realm, soon you will wear the crown."

The next day, I stood on the veranda overlooking the City of the Realm, just as my father used to do. I gazed down at my tunic. Holding onto the medallion pendant of King hanging about my neck. I Looked down at the large crowd below, as the sound of their cheers fell faint against my ears. The heavy reality of my new-found rulership could not drag my mind away from the fond memory of my father. Sadness filled my heart. He would not be here to rejoice in my ascension to the throne. I waved at the crowd, pondering my responsibility and the dubious nature of my future.

The first Council meeting, since my coronation as King, met at the City of the Realm Rotunda, adjacent to the Royal Citadel. Upon entering the room, the atmosphere bristled with antagonism and anxiety. In the middle, sat a large oval stone slab made of a conglomerate of Basta (a granite like material) embedded with striations of Auriculum (a mineral we found to amplify subtle energies of the mind).

Three pillars supported the Basta slab. The center pillar was smooth and engraved with the names of the six clans. Also inscribed on protruding bands around its periphery, were those who served on the council who had passed. The three pillars, also made of Basta, symbolized the bringer of light, the One, and the two outer pillars on each end of the oval represented the two great orbs, Liloth and Raika.

The two outer pillars, in contrast with the smooth inner pillar, had spiral grooves beginning at the top and ending in troughs at their base. Each pillar spiral turned opposite to the other. Seawater from the inlet sea poured through these channeled spirals in the same way as the pillars constructed at the entrance to the City of the Realm Temple.

Our engineers and priests determined that counter rotating seawater running against the Auriculum striations, created a balance of the Natural Forces from the earth and thus encouraged a balance of forces within the structure where they stood.

The Council room was essentially a round building with sloping walls tapering toward a domed ceiling, typical of Atlantean Architecture. The concept of open and free energy entering and exiting a structure was universal. Entrance to the rooms was gradual, so as not to disturb the energy of a room abruptly, as a spiral running along the inner wall until it opened into the main chamber. I always enjoyed the sound of the Council room, it was almost melodic even though those present would argue heatedly from time to time.

As the new King, the meeting was called to order as the overseer/priest Galmutin, pounded his staff upon the floor. The first order of business related to a change of Regent Advisor. Galmutin had been my father's Regent Advisor for hundreds of years, but I did not trust him as my confidant. Instead, I wanted another overseer/priest as my confidant. When I asked that his name be stricken from the scrolls as Regent Advisor, Galmutin stood up with outrage. I ignored his protest and continued.

"Members of this great Council…Raag began…I wish to put forth my bid for a new Regent Advisor."

An immediate discussion erupted among the governors. Then Raag pointed toward the overseer/priest standing just behind him.

"I declare Yokar, priest and overseer from the Tasher Clan as my Regent Advisor. My reasons for this choice; I believe trust is the most important shape of an advisor, an overseer as Regent Advisor is the most logical choice, they always speak with the truth of the One. To rule fairly, in this great empire, I believe my reign should be marked with that shape. Does anyone dare to challenge the logic of my decision?" Raag said, with firmness and the passion of a warrior.

Raag knew that his decision would ultimately cause some division of loyalty in the Council. Some of the regional governors admired Galmutin believing he had their interests at heart in matters of the body politic and their respective regions.

The regional governors each possessed a small scepter, reflecting insignias of their region. When a vote was called for, they would place the tapered end of the scepter into small sockets bored into the slab in front of them. Each socket reflected their vote as either a yea or nea.

Raag looked about the table to see all had placed their scepters in the yea socket save one, Galmutin. Their vote of 5 out of 6 was accepted as a vote to concede to Raag's choice of Regent Advisor.

Raag sat at the head of the oval table to the North, the position of ultimate authority and said.

"All right then…Let us begin with the business at hand, the Lemurian problem."

Galmutin stood and proclaimed.

"Raag you are a disgrace to the throne of Atlantis. You have no more right to lead this kingdom than the Lemurian warrior you butchered before this Council. You really believe your meager attempt to win the trust and soul of this Council is achieved by your fight against a

Lemurian halfling. If you had taken on a Tec for your troubles, I might have conceded your challenge. You desecrated the honor of your father by using such a poor excuse with a Lemurian surrogate!"

Raag defended.

"Galmutin…I have taken the throne as my father would have expected of me. As a warrior… an Atlantean Warrior…Yes, my opponent was a halfling Lemurian, however, his cunning and deceit bore witness to the cunning and deceit that exists amongst this Council.

Raag replied.

"I have it on good counsel that you… Galmutin…Regional Governor of the Baal Clan, sought to assassinate my father while on his hunt for the Cahwyll, but your attempts to eliminate the King failed and the fate of the One brought an untimely but natural end to my father's rule. Then, after that attempt failed, you conspired with Lemurian assassins again, to murder me as well, before I could ascend as rightful heir and Sovergn of the Realm."

Raag went on.

"What do you say to this accusation?"

Galmutin was silent for a moment…considering whether or not to admit his deceitful and nefarious deeds.

"You single me out as the bearer of the darkest shape, but I tell you, I did not act alone. There are others here who conspired with this dark plan. I would have hoped they would have the spine and fortitude to stand with me here and now.

Alas, this calamity of errors is not of their shape but mine, for trusting in their resolve and determination. You can do with me what you will, but this is far from being over and done with. I promise you, by the will of Heraklion, our god of justice, there will be another to bring the realm to reset in good course. The shape of the future will be taken from your hands, deposited into the hands of the one who holds true the devotion to the Atlantean way."

Then Galmutin went on.

"By right of my hundreds of years of service to this august body politic, I demand to know the name of my accuser?"

Yokar moved in front of the king and

proclaimed.

"I am Yokar, the King's Regent Advisor. Before this, I am Overseer and High Priest of the Temple of Appolon, the God of Knowledge, Truth and Righteousness. I am the accuser! My agents spoke to me of your treachery. You alone bring great shame and dishonor to this body politic.

"By order of the King, you are banished from the City of the Realm henceforth. Out of respect to your clan and prior governorship, your life has been spared from the torment of dismemberment of your treacherous body and fed to the jaws of a Trok."

Tec warriors escorted Galmutin from the council room in chains. He was taken to the outer walls of the City of the Realm, his chains removed, along with the medallion of governorship ripped away from his neck. The Tec warriors threw him to the ground. The massive metal gates closed with a thunderous clang, followed by the sound of the inner latch falling into the secured pockets accentuating the finality of his sentence.

Meanwhile, the remaining governors sat down at the oval table and listened quietly to Raag opening the discussion for a new treaty with the land of Mu.

Raag scanned those sitting around him for their reactions to his proclamation.

One by one, the governors placed their scepter into the yea pockets. Then Raag continued.

"Our treaty would stipulate that passage to the lands of the western shores would be allowed only by merchant traders authorized to trade. Further, that traded goods from Mu would be taxed in addition to a yearly tribute as payment for their safe passage on Atlantean territorial soil and Atlantean territorial waters.

Furthermore, the waters beyond the inlet sea, westward would be considered Atlantean territorial waters, extending to 100 leagues within the Lemurian Eastern shoreline and Eastward 200 leagues beyond the Pillars of Hercules. Raag then assigned emissaries to bring the edicts to Mu.

Then Raag stated.

"Now to more domestic issues."

Falmot, Regional Governor of the Saliene clan and Agualar Regional Governor of the Faeylan Clan were in dispute.

Falmot argued.

"Sire…The cattle belonging to my clan were being summarily slaughtered by Agualar's men while crossing over our lands to the western shores without first requesting approval of their poaching."

Agualar then stood and to defend.

"Sire…My men are fishermen. The lands to the west are broad and difficult to cross, requiring many days of travel. They cannot provide enough provisions carried with them for the journey as well as, the boats for fishing when they arrive. Without those provisions, they are too weak to deal with the transport of the fishing boats and then to fish on the sea. On return, the passage again is long and arduous. Carrying the boats and our catch from the sea, without the additional animals to eat, they will not be able to fill the City of the Realm's coffers with the fish in adequate quantities to feed the people without rest and provisions along the way."

Raag paused to consider the problem. He sat quietly and looked down at his Regal tunic pensively. Then he motioned for the Regent

Advisor to approach for consultation.

He whispered to Yokar.

'It seems to be a conundrum! I do not have a good answer for either of them Yokar. What shall I say to them?'

Yokar stroked his long white beard to ponder the problem and a possible solution. Then he placed his hand on Raag's shoulder.

"Sire…he said quietly…Perhaps the answer lies within both of their arguments.

I recommend that the fishing boats be permanently deposited near the western shores, eliminating the need to take their boats with them on their journey. Then, I would suggest that an arrangement be settled between Falmot and Agualar to barter the fish for an equal value of animals to feed the fishermen during their journeys."

Raag grinned at Yokar's wisdom. He said.

"It's good that I chose such a wise master to guide me in my internal affairs."

Then Raag turned to Agualar and Falmot.

"Agualar you will make a special journey to bring your fishing boats to the western shores where you will keep them permanently. Falmot you and Agualar will strike an agreement to barter the fish and your animals as an equal trade."

Agualar and Falmot placed their scepters in the yea pockets on the oval table.

Raag turned to yokar and nodded.

Yokar then declared.

"All business of the realm is concluded for this day; the Sovergn will retire to rest."

All the governors stood to give way to Raag's leaving the Council chamber. The rest followed out one after the other.

When Raag returned to the Sovergn's quarters in the Citadel, Yokar followed him. Raag approached the veranda. He looked out onto the City of the Realm and beyond to the inlet sea. Then he spoke softly.

Yokar, it's not what I thought it would be like. It's different than when I watched my father rule. Am I the right choice for the ruler of Atlantis?"

Yokar placed his hand on Raag's shoulder, as his father used to do. Then spoke.

"Raag…you are a fine warrior and wise beyond your years. It's unfortunate that your father could not see you now. It's what he always envisioned.

"You are doing just fine. Remember, this is your first day as King. You are off to a good beginning."

Raag continued.

"Yokar…do you not wonder about the incident with my father being bitten by the Cahwyll, when it was also planned to assassinate the King by poisoning the hunting party?"

Yokar explained.

"Raag…it is fruitless to consider this…when clearly your father's time on the throne was clearly done…and decreed by the gods, not Galmutin. His treachery therefore divided from the fate of your father. In truth, I believe it was your time to rule… as was your defeat of the Lemurian…which if I recall, was a bit touch and go from time to time!"

Raag replied.

"You are right about that…I was caught off guard with their ability to disappear by virtue of their mind control. I adapted quickly and won the day."

Yokar added.

"That's right my young King…and that you

should remember and focus on, not the fate of your father's undoing."

From our earliest origins, according to the Atlantean record keepers' accounts, the lights in the night skies have always been a source of wonder and mystery. The Tasher Clan became the watchers, the Priests and the Diviners of heavenly meanings. Thus, it began in the temples. We knew that our fate lay in the stars. That idea took hold and we began to consider our offspring as not our own.

Oh yes, for a short time, the early years of each child of Atlantis was managed by the Mother of the waters of Ma-At, and the goddess Nefrit, Goddess of Birth and Death in the hatcheries.

Over many millennia, the priests divined that birthing time was not involved with the conception time of souls. Birthing could be random, based on many unforeseen events, but conception was different, it could be predetermined.

Conception was determined by the arrangement of star patterns and those star patterns moved about the heavens as a great wheel moves, inscribing the precise formulation of conception, describing the identity and purpose of each soul, on the journey along that great wheel.

We called this cycle the Wheel of Zakeel. Within the wheel, there were gods existing, each holding their own position of importance, within the cycles of life and death. 12 positions divided into quadrants of four periods, defining the four seasons following the passage of the One through the year.

A complete cycle of the Zakeel lasted 25,772 years, symbolized by a sea serpent coiled into a circle and devouring its tail. This symbol was carved into the stone lentil above the temple head stone, at the entrance of the temples.

In Atlantis, children were not born at random, but chosen and conceived by the priesthood in accordance with the great wheel. If a Lawgiver was required, a conception was created for that, if a Craftsman was needed, another conception was created for that, and so on.

One fateful night, of the third day of the first position of Aihus, a great and wonderous star appeared, never seen before by the gazers. The presence of this special light both fascinated and frightened the priests of the temple. The priesthood arrived at the Citadel beckoning for an audience with the King.

Yokar bid them to enter the Sovergn's chamber.

Raag entered and sat upon the throne to greet them.

"What brings you to my presence at this late hour?"

The High Priest Androjin spoke first.

"Sire…we have an urgent message for you…a matter of utmost importance and urgency. We are frightened of this omen, and feel it may be the portent of some dark fate about to descend upon our world." The priest said nervously.

The second priest added.

"Our observations are too weak to determine precisely its passage and direction. We need the assistance of the makers to help us construct a monocle of light by the force of the dark attractive, giving strength beyond our capacity to see with our own eyes. We have divined an apparatus that will allow our eyes to see more."

The third priest held in his hand, a rolled parchment made from pounded Popul leaves. He unfurled the parchment to reveal the design of a most strange instrument conceived and drawn by a quill dipped in the blood from a Cahwyll.

The instrument was carved from the trunk of a Bidi tree, hollowed out and fitted with three rings of Auriculum, separated by two rings made of Ferenge powder(Iron) baked in the rays of the One. When complete, it offered the observer the power to magnify the starry spectacle, bringing the sight of it within reach with much more clarity.

Raag stared at the drawing with amazement and questioned the High priest.

"Is such a device to be made by the Baal tribe, possible?"

The High Priest Androjin answered.

"Oh yes sire…if you will ordain its manufacture, with your blessing, we could have it by the passing of the orbit of Raika. We need your sanction sire. If you will imprint your Sovergn Ring of authority upon the parchment, this will convince the makers to agree to our demands."

Raag pulled back the sleeve of his tunic, revealing the Signet Ring of authority on his forefinger. He put a short stalk of Punja, a waxy root mixed with Ferenge powder to darken its color, into the flame of an oil lamp, heating it until softened. When it was warm enough, Raag smeared the stalk upon the parchment and pressed his ring into the darkened wax.

"There…he said with a smile. Go now and make this wondrous instrument and report your findings to me with haste." Raag demanded.

The priest contingent scurried from the King's chamber leaving the citadel quickly. They mounted Quanahs and disappeared into the night, heading for the lower foothills of Scartera. There, the Baal clan lived, the village of the makers.

****

The chief scientist in the People's Center for Science, appeared at the door of the Semptor, the People's Government Authority.

"Sir…I believe we have a serious problem."

The Semptor replied.

"What is it Kal?... I have many considerations on my desk and little time for more of your rantings of disaster."

Kal stood fast with his insistence to speak.

"I know you've tolerated my alarming

confrontations in the past brother, but this is different!"

The Semptor frowned with impatience.

"All right…what is it this time?"

Kal continued.

" I've been monitoring the radiation readings picked up from the dwarf star Sirius B…and…"

Semptor responded with more impatience.

"Yes…so…speak man…I'm busy!"

Kal went on.

"Well…it's just that the radiation readings are spiking more than usual…and well…I believe it may be serious"

Semptor spoke with more agitation.

"That does not seem unusual, after all, the radiation coming from the dwarf already determined last month by the Council of Astrophysics, to be within nominal amounts."

Kal continued.

"Yes… That's true, however, the orbital oscillations have increased indicating a certain instability of the star."

"Kal…The Semptor added …I believe my brother has exhausted himself with this obsession.

I believe my brother needs to go to his quarters and increase his sleep induction tablets!"

Three days passed and the second star, Sirius A began to wobble wildly upon its axis, followed by a sudden massive burst of coronal ejected mass and gamma radiation. The flash of blue white light engulfed the nearby planets including Cannis Prime, the home world of the Aleon civilization.

The Council of Astrophysics called an emergency meeting with the Center for Government Affairs Council.

The Chief Scientist, Turkal, stood before the Council with grim news.

"Gentlemen…according to our geological findings and the medical division's report…our world is doomed. The medical doctors are receiving hundreds of female patients daily with strange symptoms, it appears that the dwarf star has emitted a vast plume of radiological particles combined with strong gamma rays and it is devastating to our women and the planet.

"Our charting of this disaster indicates, that within a singular month of time, all of our women will be gone. We are doomed to genocide. That is not the worst of the situation. The coronal ejection mass has apparently loosened the binding elements of the planet's crust. Our home world, Cannis Prime will implode within the year."

One of the council members, Kaleb, replied.

"Are these finding absolute, is there no solution to this calamity?"

Turkal replied.

"I'm afraid not! Our findings are definite. We are facing an extinction event!
We are already looking at the possibility of an evacuation of our world."

Then another council member, Teal, stood and declared.

"But where could we go? ...We have little time to prepare!"

Our team is already scanning other star systems with potential to support our people. We must begin immediately to build craft with interstellar capability."

Then another Council member, Voga, replied.

"But we do not have that ability…at best… the concepts of deep space transport remains experimental…yes?"

Turkal replied.

"It's true… the craft and propulsion for interstellar transport is experimental. Be that as it may, we have no other choice but to begin immediately, building the fleet to take our people off world. It will be risky at best.

Turkal added…

"Unfortunately, the fleet will be limited to removing only key personnel, our scientists, medical people and perhaps 200 of our most healthy men that are profiled to survive the long journey into deep space. The choice from the general populace will be by lots. I'm sorry gentlemen, we have no alternative."

***

Androjin was looking through the viewing port of the newly manufactured Star Scope. He was spanning the heavens and crossed into the Orion nebula. A bright flash of light appeared suddenly. He leaned back for a moment and rubbed his eyes.

Another priest/gazer turned from recording sightings they observed in the Lyra constellation.

He inquired with concern.

"Holy father, is there something wrong sire?" Androjin responded.

"I'm not sure, there was a bright flash of light from the warrior star, maybe the gods are angry with us for peering into their affairs too closely."

Androjin returned to the viewing port. He looked closely and could not believe his eyes. The warrior star burst into many tiny lights spreading out into the night sky. Androjin, alarmed by this sight declared.

"We must seek counsel from the king. The gods may be coming to punish us! Prepare our Quanahs for travel at once."

The other gazer replied.

"Yes, your imminence, at once."

The trio of priests arrived at the City of the Realm late the next morning. Demanding the Tec guards open the main gate. They yelled.

"We seek an audience with King Raag immediately!"

The guards yelled to the gate keepers.

"Open the gate, let the priests in."

The three Quanahs lumbered slowly into the

center of the court and stopped to allow the priest-gazers to dismount. They rushed along the outer staircase of the citadel toward the King's chamber.

Yokar stood at the entrance of the chamber.

"What is your business?" He asked.

Androjin responded out of breath from the climb.

"Please… Overseer, we must speak with King Raag immediately…it is most urgent!"

Yokar…paused to scan them with his staff. The staff vibrated with truth.

"I see your shape rings truth, you may enter."

Raag already sitting on the throne, greeted the priest-gazers with a wave of his hand, while they entered the chamber. They gave fealty, dropping to one knee as they approached the throne.

Androjin spoke first.

"Sire… We bring urgent news from the visions we have captured from the viewing port."

Raag answered with a smile.

"Good…it has been a year since we last spoke of your intentions. We take it your device works well with the heavens?"

Androjin replied.

"Oh yes Sire…very well indeed. The Star Scope works quite well and has already improved our understanding of the movements of the gods within Ma-At.

However, something has happened Sire, which we cannot explain. It is possible we may have offended the gods in our pursuit of their abodes."

Raag sat up and leaned forward with greater interest.

"So… what is this about…Do you think your device has angered the gods?"

Androjin went on.

"Last night I was viewing in the constellation of the great warrior star, and suddenly a brilliant flash of its light came across my eyes almost blinding my sight for a moment.

Then to my amazement…the warrior star emitted many tiny lights spreading out as a Cahwyll spreads its wings. As I continued to watch these tiny lights, they began to grow in their individual brightness. I believe these strange lights are coming to the earth Sire…I am frightened that the great warrior star seeks revenge for our intrusion and sent his army to attack our world!"

***

The Captain and the Navigator, looked over his console studying the star charts.

The Navigator said.

"Captain, I believe we have identified a star system that may very well suit our needs."

The Captain responded.

"I am relieved. We have been searching now for two years without much success."

"It's a binary system like ours, but its second star is much smaller. There are several planets revolving around the larger yellow star, the younger star. Of the planets in orbit, only two show promise, a blue watery planet in the third orbit and a red planet in the fifth orbit. The red planet does not indicate any sentient life, but the blue planet has many lifeforms on the surface. There also seems to be rudimentary primitive colonies on two of the land masses."

The Captain ordered.

"Navigator, plot a landing coordinate within the

area near that primitive colony. Prepare the landing party with universal translators. Hopefully, these creatures can speak some sort of intelligent language we can decipher?"

The Antares began a slow descent, as its outer hull vibrated multiple colors indicating a change in magnetic field strength. As the craft came closer to the surface, thrusters provided support until the landing pilons emerged allowing the craft to sit comfortably on the ground.

The weight of the ship brought the pilons to settle deep into the soil. As the crystal propulsion system wound down its stabilizers, the hull sat quietly illuminated by the yellow light of the One, reflecting a dull gray metallic surface.

The seamless surface of the ship's hull, began to separate exposing an inner hatch. The hatch hissed and hummed as it opened to the outside atmosphere.

The earth's atmosphere was much more enriched with Nitrogen than Cannis Prime, but well within tolerable limits.

The Aleon crew emerged to find a host of Atlantean warriors surrounding the craft and poised for battle.

The Captain switched on his translator.

"We come in peace and good will."

The warriors raised their weapons in readiness for a fight. Then the Captain turned to his First Officer.

"Well, our engineers are going to have a good time correcting our translator algorithms to adjust for these creatures. For now, we will use sign language."

Then the Captain raised his hands in the air, to the combatants in front of him signaling some sort of submission.

Word of the outworlder's arrival came quickly to the Citadel. Raag wanted to investigate. The Priesthood were terrified. They believed the warrior God sent the strangers to destroy the kingdom. When Raag arrived, mounted on his Quanah, He took one look at the Antares and dismounted his Quanah.

The Captain was armed, but he cautiously hesitated to raise his weapon. He knew, firing his weapon would only frighten the creatures more. Both sides stood several leagues apart in silence. Raag, more curious than frightened, approached with his hand on his knife for good measure, speaking to the Captain.

"Who are you? Where do you come from?"...he said with concern.

The Captain looked puzzled. He surmised quickly that Raag bore some aspect of leadership among this colony of primitives. To him, Raag seemed to be a creature of reason. As Raag tried to understand the strange sounds coming from the Captain. Raag was nervous but felt the outworlder's shape to be sincere.

The Captain dialed coordinates for his translator

to communicate with the ship's computer. He held the translator toward Raag's face. Raag tilted his head and stared at the small box in the Captain's hand.

Then Raag walked around the Captain, eyeing his clothing and physical appearance. *'A simple task of evaluating another depends on what the other wears and how strong is that one's strength.*

Aleons' were tall and slender in build. Their hands large, with 6 fingers, not five, as did the Atlanteans. The Captain's eyes were large and oval shaped with large black pupils. Their appearance seemed soft and watery with a distinct friendly gaze.

The nose was long and flattened against their cheekbones. Their heads, slightly larger, but not like a Lemurian. Their heads were high domed and presented an elongated fore brow, made exaggerated by how their eyes buried deep into their skull.

Their skin was pale and almost white, as if they never experienced the light of the One. Compared to the ruddy red tone of an Atlantean, Raag thought… *'they might be ill in some way'.*

The Captain placed his fingers against his mouth and pointed to the box. Then he pointed to Raag, motioning to his mouth and also pointing to the box. At first, this motion confused Raag. Despite the warnings of his gazers, he became attentive and copied the captain's motions. The Captain looked disappointed.

Then, the Captain spoke into the box, asking the computer to repeat his words. When the box announced the Captain's words, everyone jumped back with wonder except Raag. One priest blurted out.

"How could someone live inside such a small box?"

To them, it seemed like magic! Raag was pragmatic and practical, as was his father, the king.

Despite his better judgement, he voted against the colony's distrust and boldly approached the Captain. Raag pointed to the box and then to his mouth and waited for a response from the Captain.

The Captain jerked back slightly, stunned by Raag's boldness. He felt foolish for a moment, then he recovered and began to study Raag more closely. The Captain wondered, *'perhaps these people are not truly as primitive as they believed them to be.'* In the next moment, the Captain looked at Raag directly with a slight smile. Spontaneously, Raag returned with his smile.

The Captain pressed the echo button on the translator and handed the box to Raag. He held it for a moment, checking the surface quality, how smooth and perfectly shaped the box felt. Then he believed he was talking with a God. One who came from the lights in the sky.

Suddenly Raag became filled with excitement about the idea he would have the privilege to commune with the gods. Next, he pulled the box closer and spoke; 'I do not understand you. We need to communicate.' Moments later, after a period of silence, the box repeated Raag's words replaying his voice.

The Tec Warriors, Noblemen and Law Givers moved back several paces aghast at what they saw…It seemed a terrible choice to be made, because many believed first, that the King would now choose to support the strangers more than the colony. On the other hand, the colony may believe the King has been secretly mesmerized in some magical way by the outworlder and he is not himself.

Then they believed that the box was a magical prison and Raag's soul is captured within! There arose so much clamor and controversy that Raag quickly offered to return the box.

The Captain returned to the ship with his first Officer in tow leaving the hatch door to close behind them. Once inside the control room, he turned and said to the Navigator.

"We are going to need to analyze that creature's sounds. How quickly can we develop an algorithm to solve this dilemma?

The Philologist standing by suggested. "The ship's computer already possesses our language base. If we can obtain a map of their sounds it would be easy and take only a few hours. My concern is; with that little exposure to their sounds may not be enough for the computer to solve the puzzle."

"Understood…said the Captain…if we can obtain some base from the computer, it might be easier in the next exposure. In this case, if we don't get it this time, then next time we will."

The excitement soon dwindled and not many remained nearby the vessel.

Raag returned to his chamber in the Citadel. He closed the inner doors for privacy.

He opened his sash revealing he possessed the mysterious box. He placed the box on the shelf nearby, staring at it for several minutes. The feeling when he first touched it still lingered in his mind. Eventually, the wonderful experience overpowered his reluctance, he pick it up and held it in his hands.

As his hands rubbed the surface, he realized that the box wasn't so smooth, but the invisible field around it buzzed so minutely and quietly that it would disguise the surface with a shield of buzzing energy. The pleasant feeling returned again as he kept moving it through his fingers. Feeling a bit more comfortable with this strange new toy, he began to explore all of its features.

At the end of the box several buttons protruded beyond the surface. There were strange characters near each button. His curiosity overwhelmed him. He began pressing each button watching for a result.

There was little to advance Raag's success at solving this most strange puzzle.

After trying every button, he became frustrated and began pressing more than one button at a time.

After several experimental tries, the third combination was a shock, Raag managed to activate the box's ability to function as a communication device. Moreover, the combination he stumbled upon was a ship-wide access to the vessel. He began to speak, not realizing he was spreading his voice throughout the ship.

The Captain jumped from his seat and said.

"Oh no, I left my translator with the creature. The bad news is, he has my translator. The good news is, he has figured out how to use it. Which, confirms my original contention; these people are not primitive, just raw untrained intelligence."

The Navigator told the Philologist he needed to store the creatures sounds, for as long as it was available. Hours later, the laboratory aboard the ship had compiled sufficient sounds and their derivatives and provided those files to the ship's computer. With that data, the ship's computer successfully created the translation keycode for the

Atlantean dialect. As soon as the Captain learned of the engineer's success, he immediately ordered his translator to be upgraded to resume his conversations with the creature.

It was the morning of the next day. The Captain opened the hatch of the craft, and stepped out of the ship. He hopped briefly to the ground while clutching the new translator, he spoke to those around him.

"Greetings to you, we have come here to greet you and share in the peaceful pursuits between us." The message kept repeating until it reached the halls of the Citadel in the City of the Realm.

Yokar knocked on Raag's chamber door to reveal the news.

"The 'newcomers' can speak our language!" Raag quickly prepared to journey back to the vessel still sitting where it had landed.

When Raag arrived and dismounted his Quanah, he found the Captain of the Antares standing outside of the ship, holding a second translator.

Raag approached extending an outreached arm holding the original translator in his hand.

As Raag handed over the original translator, the Captain spoke through the translator, but this time the box did not repeat his words but emitted words in Raag's tongue.

"Greetings to you, we come bearing gifts and peaceful intentions. We mean you no harm."

Raag, taken back by the stranger speaking his language, felt speechless. Moments later, he recovered and responded.

"We call our world Atlantis, I am King and leader of this land and have many questions for the outworlders from the lights in the sky. Why do you come here?

My priests say you are the gods of the warrior star here to punish us. I can see your true shape, so lying will be evident."

The Captain paused to answer quickly. This opportunity would define how future negotiations might unfold, so he wanted to embrace the creature's perspective before he answered his questions.

"I come from a star system, and a planet that revolves around that star, much in the same way the bodies we call moons, revolve around your planet as well as, this planet revolves around your star. We have come to you because we have spent many years searching the heavens for a solution to our problem, a problem that spells certain extinction for our people. We think that your people may be able to help us overcome this problem to survive."

Raag hesitated because though he could understand the Captain's words now, many terms still puzzled his mind. Then he continued.

"Please explain your problem quickly as my people are anxious about your arrival. They are frightened by your ways. This vessel you traveled on, a most strange device, something we have never experienced in our world. We have no means to fly here. It is our belief flying is left for those creatures that possess wings to do so. We are without wings, so we believe that flying is forbidden for us, by the One, the Light Giver."

The Captain took more time to embrace the expressed philosophy given by Raag. Having knowledge of other civilizations of a primitive nature, he could understand and tolerate the beliefs and superstitions presented by those primitive cultures. Then he added.

"We come to provide aid to your people in any way we can, using our knowledge and ways. In exchange, we want to understand your ways and find a way that we can merge our way with your way, so both peoples can enjoy the fruits of our joint efforts."

Raag spoke again.

"So, you want to trade with us…we have nothing that can compare to the wonders you offer. What would you find helpful from our people to your people?"

The Captain said.

"I think before we talk about trading, we should come together and share together what we are about, what we could do for you and learn what your culture is about as well as, some of your needs. Then we can talk more of trading. We are also interested to learn about cultures different from us, it will benefit us to know about your way, and your world."

Raag turned to Yokar. He felt his wisdom to respond in the right way would be essential. Yokar spoke.

"King, as Sovergn of the Realm, you will face the problem of negotiating with different peoples, with different cultures, not unlike the Lemurians. Perhaps it is wise to listen from these strangers. Take notice of their different way, which may in turn, provide insight, to increase your knowledge and wisdom to guide your people more effectively."

Raag trusted Yokar and his great wisdom as an Overseer and as his confidant.

He turned to the Captain and replied.

"My Council has given me cause to accept your offer to meet and discuss our different ways together. I feel you are the supreme leader of your people as I am also for my people.

"You will come first, with some of your trusted counsel to the City of the Realm, to the Citadel, there we will share food and drink and discuss many things. We have Quanahs for our transportation, I think you will need to use your own ways to navigate the terrain. These creatures are difficult to manage even by those more experienced."

The Captain smiled and agreed. He turned to

his First Officer and commanded.

"Number One, break out the speeders and bring provisions enough to carry four of us. We will follow them slowly to their abode they call the City." Set the ship's computer and the rest of the crew on standby in our absence. We will maintain continued communications with the ship and crew for any updates."

The Antares bay doors hummed to open, exposing smaller craft capable of land travel as well as, water transport where needed. The craft, the Aleons called a speeder, revealed a flattened deck hollowed out for seating and a control console mounted forward, with an aero-aquatic dynamic shape and powered by their magnetic repulsor. When engaged, allows the craft to float some feet from the surface of any ground or above any water. The throttle mechanism was like a power management system controlling elevation as well as, navigating the terrain in any direction.

As the Quanahs lumbered toward the City of the Realm, the speeders followed. Raag entered the King's chamber where sat the throne of the King. The Captain and his entourage entered and stood by while Raag ordered the court attendants to bring seating for his guests, in addition he ordered plates of Soab and urns of fermented Scawberry.

Raag tipped his cup and said to the Captain.

This is our choice of drink, it is a mild fermented liquid made from the juice of Scawberrys hand-picked by our farmers of the Realm.

The Captain looked around scanning the unusual Atlantean architecture and commented.

"Your buildings are of an unusual shape and design. They seem soothing to the eye and open to the natural surroundings. You do not have pests or small creatures running about inside, yet we see them plentiful in the fields on the way to your castle in the city. How do you keep them from interfering with your daily life?"

Raag replied.

"We are relaxed with their presence. They are harmless creatures for the most part, so we do not concern ourselves. Yet, I must admit, the pleasant scent of the Bidi leaves you may have detected upon entering, act as a mild deterrent to their invasion our living space. They do not care for the unique sweet smell, it becomes an irritant to their breathing. They are satisfied with roaming the outer courtyards and content not to enter where it is uncomfortable."

The Captain replied.

"I see…he said, as he tilted his cup of juice and sipped on it…hmm"… he mumbled as he looked at Raag, waiting for his response to the drink.

Raag said with a challenge.

"You do not favor our choice of drink?"

The Captain took another larger sip of the juice and replied.

"Well, I am not accustomed to drinking fermented substances, it is not recommended for our form of travel among the stars. Let's just say, while I'm in your gracious setting, I will adjust. Perhaps, I will have a stronger liking later."

Raag smiled.

"Your shape is true…I think we will enjoy your gratitude at a later date then."

Then Raag shifted his mood to establish a deeper understanding of his strange guests.

"You have a name…more than your title as

leader of your clan?"

The Captain expressed a little regret.

"I'm very sorry…How rude of me…My name is Adalon. I am Captain of my ship, the Antares. My people are called Aleons. We come from a world known as Cannis Prime, a planet that encircled the larger of two stars called Sirius A and B."

Adalon continued.

"In fact, we are refugees from our planet, a world that was dying. Our females have all succumbed to a massive surge of deadly energy our star gave forth unexpectedly."

"So, your light giver has become angry with you and punishes you for your actions!" Raag Blurted out.

Adalon smiled at Raag's remark.

"Well…One might say that. We are a technological race of people who have developed ways to understand Natural Forces. We feel differently about such matters. It's not that we have done anything wrong to offend our star, but the energy of our star does not reflect our spiritual or moral ethics. Rather, simply an unfortunate occurrence where our star came to the end of its existence. We happened to be at the wrong place at the wrong time."

Raag leaned forward for a moment to enquire.

"What is this technological quality of your people?"

Adalon answered.

"It's our way that we have developed to handle the Natural Forces that exist. We have gone beyond building fires to warm our bodies, we have stopped using fire to light our dwellings. We have no longer the need to place beasts of burden to transport us where we want to go. Instead, we use technology to do all of that for us, leaving time for us to pursue other activities more pleasing to us.

"The way of technology allows us to float above the ground like our speeders that brought us to the castle in the city. It is the way technology allows our ships to travel quickly through the stars and brought us here to your world.

"It is the way of technology that prevents the ravages of disease which used to plague our people a long time ago. Now we enjoy long life as well as, excellent health. Our doctors are very skilled with the nature of the physical body. We can use technology to correct those defects that might arise through the birthing when needed.

Raag looked puzzled.

"So, the gods have given you powers that they alone wield, powers that make you equal to them?"

Adalon replied.

"Well…we are not gods. Perhaps we appear as gods to you only because you do not have technology yet. Someday, in your future, your people could do as we do, command and control your world, far more effectively than you do now.

Raag inquired again.

"So, with the power you wield, why could you not save your world and make peace with your star?"

Adalon replied.

"King Raag, even with our enormous technological knowledge and skill, that was impossible for us to handle. Perhaps in the future, when our people can thrive again, we will be able to control the light and heat of a star, but that is not now, at this time. First, we must find a solution to our real dilemma…we have no women to repopulate our clan, as you would call it. That is why we are here. We need your help."

Raag again looked at Adalon with a furrowed brow.

"So, how is it that an inferior Atlantean culture is capable of helping the gods?"

Adalon said slowly.

"We wanted to bargain for some of your women, to experiment with, in our laboratories."

Raag replied.

"What is a laboratory?

Adalon answered.

"A laboratory is where we have much technology collected, along with much knowledge of the physical body to find the solution to our problem. We cannot use our men for such experiments, there are too few of us, and we need females to be the source of the solution."

Raag argued.

"It seems perfectly clear to me, our women are quite different than your people. How is it they could be of any help to solving your problem?"

Adalon answered.

"We have the power to change your women, to

alter their bodies to be much more alike to our kind. With that done, we could bring them with us to where we will go. Then we could procreate greater numbers, so that our clan will survive."

Raag paused for a moment before answering.

"If this is what you require, then what will you give our clan to help us?"

Adalon spoke more excited.

"We could share our knowledge and technology, teach your people how to use it, advance your world to make it a better and easier place to live."

Raag paused again.

"I will not give you an answer just now. I will confer with my Council. and I will bring this before the women of our tribe. We do not own our women, they belong to the whole of the tribe. We will see how they would feel about changing to another clan and another world with this experiment."

Adalon replied.

"I understand King Raag. I shall return to my ship and await your answer, so until then, we thank you for your audience and willingness to grasp our dilemma.

"We hope for our sake and yours, we can come to an agreement."

Raag replied.

"We cannot commit until my Council has decided."

After the Aleons left, Raag turned to his Regent Counselor Yokar for advice.

"Yokar…what shall I do about this most strange request? …Do you understand this 'technology' Adalon is talking about?" I need to know before I plan to bring this issue before the High Council.

Yokar replied.

"Sire…I believe the closest expression in our language is 'Techlogi'…it means 'fierce logic'. It represents a very different way of perceiving things of the world.

You must proceed with caution my King."

***

The Lemurian Council gathered together awaiting the last to arrive at the conference, that one would be Galmutin. Galmutin still harbored many feelings of regret, anger, followed by humiliation and judgement. His intent to establish a newer view of himself and his value, depended on getting attention, even if it bore negative effects.

To that end, he called a meeting with the Lemurian Council to reveal a plan for payback, for him and for the Lemurians. So he began.

"You must know, that we share a common bond. We both hate the Atlanteans, and all that they stand for."

The Lemurian leader Ligi Sumutu, the Cephalopod (octopus) challenged this idea.

"You are Atlantean! How can we trust the words of one who denies their own kind? This is like a Council divided. Nothing good will come of it. What can you offer us." Ligi Sumutu asked.

Galmutin replied.

"I have knowledge of the City of the Realm, I can guide you to the secret passages inside where the King resides. The time to strike is now. I can help you to return to your rightful place, a ruler of both worlds!"

The leader said.

"What will you require in return for your treachery?"

Galmutin answered.

"I will have satisfaction to see King Raag's world fall before him. Then I will rule the Atlantean kingdom subservient to your supreme rulership. You must act now Ligi Sumutu, this opportunity will not last!"

"If you betray us", Ligi said, "I will take great pleasure in removing your skin from your body and roasting you slowly over the fires of Balan."

The leader called forth his mighty army. Thousands marched over the land to the eastern shores of Lemuria. Hundreds of ships loaded with battle ready troops prepared for their assault on the Atlantean Realm.

Aboard the Antares, the ship's computer noted the advance of many ships arriving at the inlet sea of the City of the Realm.

"Captain…the computer began…there appears to be a hostile horde approaching from the sea. It would appear an assault is about to begin."

Captain Adalon announced to his crew, a local skirmish from another species is on its way toward the Atlantean City. If our plans for an exchange with the Atlanteans succeed, we will need to interfere. Arm yourselves with side arms and set your weapons for stun only, we have no desire to extinguish an entire species. We will engage before they reach their target."

The hatch of the Antares opened allowing 20 crew members to pour out. They formed a semi-circle in front of the ship to face the Lemurian horde approaching on Ganthas(a smaller reptile, having a thin tail, long neck and a long narrow snout, supported by long powerful legs.)

Lemurian warriors carried little in the way of weapons, counting heavily on their mind-bending skills to trick their opponents. Light weight hand axes slung over their shoulders were preferred tools for battle. Unlike Quanahs, Ganthas were exceedingly quick with their stride allowing rapid penetration of an enemy's defenses.

When the front line of the Lemurian battalion arrived, their senses could not grasp the significance of the Antares sitting directly in the way of their assault.

They halted briefly to gape at the strange

massive metallic object and the strange creatures standing in front.

Ligi Sumutu, undaunted by this obstruction, blinded by and confident of his vision of victory, ordered his soldiers to move in and attack these pitifully few creatures. The crew of the Antares open fired upon the hordes laying waste to their numbers with wide sweeping rays of light never before seen by the Lemurian army. Moments later, thousands of Lemurian soldiers lay silent on the Atlantean beachhead. Their leader and the few remaining still standing, turned and ran for their lives beating a hasty retreat into their ships.

Galmutin fearing a reprisal from the Lemurian leader, turned to escape the onslaught through the nearby forest, heading for Baal territory.

King Raag approached with Tec warriors ready for battle and shocked to see the Lemurian assault so quickly suppressed by only 20 of the Antares crew. Raag dismounted his Quanah and approached Adalon with great relief.

Raag declared.

"It would seem you have turned the tide of this battle in quick order, and with so few soldiers. So many dead!"

Adalon admitted.

"Oh… they are not dead, they are stunned by our weapons. Ready for your capture and imprisonment. We have the advantage you see, it is technology that wins the day. This kind of power over your enemies is indispensable and will ensure long lasting peace my friend."

Raag sighed.

"I am beginning to understand. We have much to discuss. I will call an immediate meeting with my Council."

A meeting of the High Council convened in the Citadel with the King, Raag presiding. The room bristled with anticipation and anxiety regarding the presence of the outworlders. Adalon sat at the table where Galmutin would've been seated. All other Regional Governors sat around him, with his First Officer and adjutant standing behind their Captain at resting attention.

Yokar pounded his staff to the floor signaling the meeting to begin. Raag spoke first.

"I realize you have many questions today. We will certainly answer as many as is deemed necessary. First, I want to introduce the leader of the outworlders, Captain Adalon, commander of his ship the Antares and two members of his crew.

"I don't have to tell you, the outworlders came to our aid yesterday with good measure. It was no contest to thwart a massive surprise attack from the Lemurian colony, led by Galmutin. That he led an insurrection to overthrow our government will be a matter we can attend to at a later time. That horde was deflected by a wonderful and quite effective demonstration of their way. Their way is called Techlogi, which means 'fierce logic' according to my Regent Counselor."

The Regional Governor Tark, of the Feylan Clan inquired.

"So, at some distance, we could see the light of the One streaming from your hands. How do you command the light of the One in this way? We have never witnessed the One to descend to our world, to assist in our conflicts before. Do you speak confidently with our god? Does that mean we are sitting together with gods from other lights in the sky?"

Raag gestured for Adalon to speak freely. Holding the translator close by, he began.

"As we told your King, we are not gods as such, but we do command the forces of Nature. We want to share our knowledge with you, in order to resolve our problem. That is why we are here at this time. We seek your help to solve our problem. We are requesting a number of your females for conducting experiments toward increasing our numbers."

Governor Tark continued.

"How many females do you want?"

"We need to procreate, and your women are not

compatible to our kind. We want to make some changes until they are compatible."

Then Adalon turned to his First Officer.

"Have we ascertained how many will be required yet?"

First Officer, Tomlin replied.

"The first estimate from our doctors is 1000 females, to begin with Sir. This number could change more or less, depending on the genetic sequence."

Adalon continued to address Raag.

"What is your average life span?"

Raag looked puzzled.

Adalon added.

"I mean, how long do your people live?"

Raag smiled joking.

"As long as possible! ...not counting mishaps, or death by combat, our expectant life duration is a thousand cycles of the One."

Now Adalon was confused.

"By your reference to the One, you mean your star. The orbital relationship of your planet? ...so, you mean 1000 years...yes?

Raag nodded in the affirmative.

Adalon again turned to the First Officer.

"Their life expectancy is 5% of ours…that could almost work."

"Contact the ship…see if that length will allow for a realistic sequencing.

Tomlin used his communicator to reach the ship's computer.

"Computer…compute the sequence required to reach ideal genetic matching of the Atlantean biological subjects to the Aleon Biologic?"

The ship's computer responded.

"Working…it is projected, with 1000 samples, will take 1000 years of permutations to reach a 92.7% near perfect sequence for successful fertilization."

"If these creatures agree, we can set up camp here for that duration. Save one or two, most of the crew have more than enough life span to complete our mission here…in time for our return to the new destination, the Pleiades Star System…Sir."

Adalon returned to Raag and extended his hand.

"Well Raag…what say you…do we have a trade?"

Raag nodded and reluctantly reached to seize

hold of Adalon's hand.

"Perfect…Adalon said with relief…we just need to pick our subjects and prepare the lab for the sequencing process to begin. I will arrange to have several communicators adapted to your lingual algorithms. Then our engineers can begin to talk your language and introduce our way to your people.

Raag considered who might be suitable for this exchange. Yokar suggested.

"The 'Makers' of the Baal clan, as a wise choice Sire… the aptitude for embracing new concepts and finding ways to adapt will be the most promising choice for the exchange."

Raag agreed, but he wanted others from other clans to try it also.

Captain Adalon added.

"First, your people will need to come aboard our ship and be prepared for intellectual acceleration. Again, it is our way. To understand our physics, our Techlogi, we will need to accelerate the mental capacity of your people.

"The process is not harmful. The process may cause some to feel an ache in the head, as the interface is not precise for your mental construct. We have a special machine for this. Everyone will need to be connected to our machine for the preparation. The time to learn will be much shorter."

Raag felt bewildered. He could only embrace some of what the Captain was talking about. He agreed provisionally to be first, waiting until the next day to experience this learning machine for himself. Once he tried the machine, he would provide a random sample of men and women from each clan to see who could handle the changes the machine would make.

It was early morning. A line of Atlantean men and women stood by waiting to enter the ship. Raag was first in line to enter. He climbed the steps leading to the hatch slowly, remembering his Counselor, *'My advice, is to move forward, but with caution.'*

The ships corridor was paved with a floor made of metal that was perforated. As he passed by each section, it would automatically illuminate, providing a pale blue light on the floor and surrounding walls. Adalon's people moved about passing Raag as though he wasn't present, performing all manner of tasks which seemed very odd to him.

Moment to moment, he would stop and stare, trying to grasp this strange alien environment. The air was strangely neutral…having no natural odor at all. The air quality seemed a bit thin, less oxygen forced his lungs to heave from time to time, to recapture what his body thought was lost. It made him a little dizzy.

Adalon conducted the initial tour of his ship. Raag could tell, he was feeling proud to show his new acquaintance his domicile and advanced transport. Adalon opened the hatchway, revealing the heart of the ship, the engine room. Raag's mouth fell open with eyes widened. Before him was a monstrous crystal glowing a phosphorescent blue color. It seemed to be suspended in a clear liquid surrounded by three metal bands glowing red like the caldera of Scartera.

The bands hummed loudly in a pulsating manner which frightened him making this part of the tour less exciting. He quickened his pace to leave the area.

Finally, he entered the control room, dazzling with all manner of blinking lights and strange active diagrams changing on the walls. In one area was a large rectangular box covered with thousands of tiny lights, running up and down and side to side in rhythmical fashion. This was the ships quantum computer. Raag was spellbound at the sight of it.

Adalon added.

This is the machine I was talking about. You will be connected to it and the machine will contact your mind and your thoughts. It will also sample a small amount of your blood for sequencing. Once it figures how you process thought, it will begin to make changes that will make you smarter, then it will start your education of our way, our Techlogi."

Raag quietly gulped. He maintained an outer veneer of calmness but he was nervous on the inside. Captain Adalon bid Raag to sit down in one of the cockpit chairs. A silver band lowered from the cabin ceiling, wrapping around Raag's head. Three large probes extended inside the band that touched Raag's head in three places, and a smaller band wrapped around his left wrist. The Captain switched on the attached equipment. A faint tingling ran through his head and body, followed by a small stinging prick of his wrist.

"The sensations you feel will not cause harm, it's the way the learning machine discovers your blood quality and your mental aptitude. Soon, after the machine learns about you, it will provide an adjustment inside your head and then the information of our way will proceed." Adalon confirmed.

Raag squirmed a little in his seat, wondering what will come next. His eyes began to close and his body relaxed. Images and information streamed into his mind with lightening speed. The computer utilized the lingual algorithms previously determined to exchange the information. A mild sedative administered at the beginning, reduced the effect of any stress caused by the transfer.

He believed the machine was a dream creating device, very similar to his dreams he enjoyed while on a hunt with his father. These dreams were strange. Unfamiliar ideas and concepts thrust into his mind, yet, though they were unfamiliar, they seemed to grow less and less disturbing. A sensation of pleasure arose in his body, similar to his experiences in the baths of isle of Tiber, a place to the south, (near what is now called Bimini) presenting many hot volcanic pools where warriors could go to heal their wounds from battle.

Raag opened his eyes feeling refreshed. He looked up to see Adalon peering down on him smiling.

"Very good my friend. The compatibility examination was a success. And certain changes have been made to allow further education. Your ability to process information is greatly enhanced. Later, as your mind continues to adapt to your newly improved intellect, you may feel a little dizzy for a while."

Adalon continued.

"This treatment is just the beginning. You will need to make several visits to the ship, continuing the process of accepting our way. You are done for now, I recommend you return to your Citadel to rest. We will continue with the other members of your council, then the other men and women too. It will provide a strong basis for evaluating the overall adaptability of your kind to our way."

Raag replied.

"Please contact me when you are finished."

On the morning of the next day, Raag called a meeting with the High Council. The atmosphere in the throne room was agitated, even hostile.

Yokar opened the meeting with his staff striking the floor of the chamber.

Before Raag could speak, Jax of the Tec clan stood and began a tirade of fear and complaint.

"Great King, I and members of my clan are here to dispute this invasion of our culture. These beings are strangers to us. They do not understand the importance of our way, the way of the One, the Law Giver. We believe this is an aberrant violation of the Natural System of things in Atlantis. This Techlogi is an abomination! We vote to stop this re-education process. We believe it is a subtle way of conquering our people with their infernal device!"

Other members of the council stood to voice similar issues of concern and agreed with Jax. Raag sat quietly, listening to their rants and waited until all had voiced their opinions. Only one said nothing during the heated discussion.

The Baal clan, now led by the new regional governor, Malgar, who sat quietly. Raag turned to Malgar.

"We hear nothing from the Baal Clan, what say you to all this?"

"Malgar declared.

"Sire, we of the Baal clan feel the new process is most profitable. We are excited that this new knowledge and mental clarity will serve to be of greater aid to all Atlantis. We are sure that the Tec Clan would agree, to have use of the Light of the One in their hands to ensure our dominant rulership of both our world and the world of the Lemurians."

Raag turned to Jax.

"Jax do you agree with Malgar, that we should not stop the trade agreement?"

Jax replied.

"Well…we are eager to add their weapons to our arsenal for sure, but as to the rest, we are fearful Sire."

"I will confer with Adalon later to find if the process is satisfactory for his needs as well. We will convene again later." Raag decreed. Then the Council disbanded, still grumbling amongst each other, as they left the Citadel.

Raag went to the Antares to speak with Adalon about the overall results of the mind machine treatment.

"Well…Adalon…what happened? …Did everyone do well with the machine?"

Adalon paused to answer.

"On average…Sire…most adapted well, but the clan you call Baal exceeded our expectations. Other than preparing the women for sequencing, that tribe should be the first to undergo the complete transfer. It's as though they are like Aleon children, eager and quick to learn…the machine gave them a better than 80 % chance to absorb our way completely.

Raag smiled.

"Makes sense! ...We call them the 'Makers'… they are very intuitive and clever at dealing with complexity. In addition, the general consensus with the Council is to vote against the trade…Adalon winced to hear those words… however…Raag continued… it is the Baal clan that voted for continuing the process. This fact gives me an opportunity to present the issues of the trade agreement with a different approach. The Baal clan was always struggling to find comfort with providing their skills to the colony. They will be pleased to be singled out, while the others will be relieved to discontinue their part in this trade."

Adalon took a deep breath of relief.

"So, the trade agreement continues, with the Baal…and what about the King, will he continue to submit to the learning machine as well?"

Raag smiled.

"Yes…our culture is dependent on their King being able to rule effectively. I do want so much to offer my best effort to enhance my mental clarity, to be a keeper of the new way for future generations. I want Atlantis to be the motherland of wealth and prosperity, holding the promise of a brighter future for our kind and for all time to come. So yes, I will continue the learning process as well. The Tec's purpose, I think, is to learn the use of your light weapons. I also agree with that idea. I want our security forces to function with greater clarity and cleverness in battle, beyond the use of the light weapons."

Adalon added.

"Raag, you are a great leader. Your people are lucky to have a wise King to lead them."

Atlantean women gathered in front of the Antares anxiously waiting for the DNA sequence process to begin. The ship's computer revealed that the women would need to be intellectually advanced first, before any DNA changes could begin.

They were excited with the process. They admired the look of Aleon women from the ship. Their hair was soft and thin, unlike the Atlantean hair, more like fur, thick and unkept. The bodily features attracted them the most. Atlantean women were built stocky and muscular, not much different than the men of Atlantis.

Compared to the Aleons, their eyes were small, round and somewhat beady in appearance. Their eye colors were all the same, a small black pupil surrounded by a sheen of amber embedded with many lighter striations streaming from the center. The most exciting part of their transformation, the journey to the home of the gods, high in the starry firmament.

What they didn't know, the DNA sequencing would not be driven, meaning it would not be something which could occur within one generation. In fact, many generations would be required. So,1000 participants over 1000 years would mean thousands of deviants, discarded along the way. Only the end group of select would travel to the stars with the Aleons.

Part of their preparation would be to shorten their life span by tenfold. That knowledge was kept from the selected members of the Baal tribe. The 1000 participants became 100,000 in effect, as they were forced to progenerate offspring by virtue of invitro fertilization for the next round of sequencing within each 100-year span.

What would happen to the discarded of this grand experiment? An issue, which would be dealt with at some later time. Raag became aware of this early on with his re-education. He did not express concern. Women were really chattel, used for work and procreation, their main contribution to the colony. They were happy to receive changes in their appearance in a much shorter period, by their standards.

On a technological level, the makers of the Baal clan engaged quickly, assimilating the knowledge at an amazing pace. Already working with the crystal technology, they learned the process of creating pure crystals with an extremely cold bath of super saturated minerals surrounded by the cold magnetic force, an idea expanded upon in their training.

The new powerful crystals could be installed in small adjustable chalices surrounded by the iron and iridium bands, stimulating infinite molecular transmutation of sunlight into localized light, heat and a form of electrical energy, the Newcomers called Neutral Force. Soon the landscape of Atlantis transformed in a short time, into a colony of advanced technology users. The application of their new-found knowledge extended into metallurgy, medical wonders and transport. Quanahs gave way to an Atlantean version of the Aleon speeder. Even sailing vessels were transformed into Atlantean vessels that could travel at greater speeds above and below the water.

After several hundred years passed, an Atlantean aerial vehicle (the Vimana) brought a new experience, flight to the Atlantean people. Visions of a greater empire, expanding to other lands as outposts, moving beyond the continent lay on the table for discussion.

The engineers developed devices that could scan deep within the crust, looking for more exotic ores to mine for all of their new projects. They also used these devices to study the volcanic conditions of their home world, providing early warning to the colony of impending eruptions. With new materials discovered almost daily, the engineers conceived of huge digging machines, to bore large holes into the crust, thinking that they could travel underground to reach other land masses.

They soon discovered the power sources for their boats, submarines and sky ships limited to short distances. The makers thought to make larger crystals but the weight was prohibitive in most cases. Then utilizing the communication concepts aboard the Antares, the makers conceived of three towers built to create a field of energy streaming within a triangulated shape from the mountain tops. The towers would be temples devoted the Law of the One.

By tuning the crystals to vibrate in unison, a standing field of energy would result, not draining the power of any craft, but resonating for the power required from the triple sources. Then all manner of transport, by sea, by land or by air could at once be powered by the One's energy with no losses. Coming to understand these laws of resonance, all manner of manufacturing would be based upon this idea of tuning.

The engineers realized that the machinery no longer deteriorated in any way, operating without normal wear and tear commonly experienced before. They realized in this discovery, the idea of a higher order of perfect harmony with all things outmatching their cruder understanding of Nature as before.

Looking to bring the experience of harmony in greater ways, deeper and more involved, brought this new Techlogi infiltrating in everyday life.

Clothing made and worn by women were adorned with very small crystals tuned to their vibrations, so while they moved about, their clothing would alight with varying colors while ringing delightful melodies reflecting the uniqueness of their personage.

It had been a little over 1000 years since the first genetic experiments began. The Aleons now had more than 300 transformed Atlantean women confirmed by the computer on board the Antares, to be well within the parameters of successful fertilization. The Newcomers, as the outworlders were now referred to, were ready to return to a new world of their own. Adalon came to the City of the Realm and entered the Citadel to request an audience with King Raag.

Yokar approached and offered to escort him to the King's chambers.

"The King is dealing with some domestic issues and will be available shortly. It is our understanding that the great task is now complete and you are ready to travel back to the stars. You mentioned a star cluster that will be your new dwelling place. Can you describe this place to me while we wait for the King to be free."

Adalon said.

"The cluster is not far, by line of sight, from the warrior's star cluster, which we call Orion's Belt. If you gaze further south to the brightest star called Aldebaran, it is a cluster of stars, counting seven in all. We have chosen either of two, a star called Taygeta and/or Merope, both are medium aged stars, having several suitable planets orbiting respectively. The planet we prefer, most closely similar to our original world does not have a name. So, our crew decided to name it Antares Prime, after our starship."

Yokar added.

"It is our wish that the travel to your new home world is a smooth journey and will bring peace and prosperity to your people, that you will flourish and repopulate in greater numbers for your tribe. Then he gestured the warrior's symbolic good will saying, ToshMalon (may all your battles be good ones)"

Adalon placed his hand across his chest gesturing a heart-felt thanks.

"We hope that our way has brought your world greater abundance and peace as well, Yokar."

Yokar excused himself to enter into the throne room. Raag concluded the business of the day and bid Adalon to enter. He turned to wave Adalon into the throne chamber.

Raag and Adalon grasped hands and forearms, as in the way of Atlantean friends and warriors, who greet each other after a long absence.

"Adalon…it's great to see you. I trust your great plan is concluded successfully and as I understand from my aides, you are preparing to leave."

Adalon responded.

"Yes…that is correct. Our ship is almost ready to leave. I must admit, I am a little sad to part from your world. In its own way, quite charming. You and I have become good friends over these many years. We will of course make a place on our world to commemorate your people helping our people to survive. You and your world will not be forgotten. Perhaps, we will return one day to see what effect we have had with what we gave you."

Raag replied.

"That would be most appreciated. Don't make it too long. After all, you live a lot longer than we… smiling, Raag said…Good bye my friend and thank you again."

Raag stood on the veranda, in the same place his father stood, so many years ago. He watched the Antares lift off in a flash of brilliant colors, changing to a light brighter than the Law Giver, the One. He followed its course into the sky until it could not be seen any longer. Raag wondered now about his realm. So many things about their culture had changed. The people of all the clans seemed to take the Techlogi in stride.

Many of the original Regional Governors have passed. They have been replaced with their younger counterparts. The energy of the High Council lost the stability he once knew. The young lords are less inclined to adapt to the old ways in favor of adopting new laws that reflect a certain recklessness.

Adalon told him the procedure with the intellectual improvements would also make changes in his DNA. His life span no longer reflects the genetic profile he once was before. Adalon went on to say… the deeper changes suggested an inconclusive number for Raag's life span. The obvious fact remains, more than a 1000 years have already passed since his first treatment. Now, there is no way to tell how long the King might live. Raag's physical appearance changed very little over that time.

Plans for construction are underway for the three temples to be built on the three mountain peaks, Scartera, Sepula and Palinor. Within the temples will house the great crystals, the Taoi stones(meaning fire stones). At the entrance of each temple, great monuments will be erected, statues of the first Law Givers of the earliest times, Kantsu and Riantsu.

Each Taoi, developed by our brilliant engineers, created in the cold baths of superconducting mercury, a white metal, phosphorite bronze, a dark red metal and magnetically charged Iridium, the second active white metal.

With hundreds of years in preparation, these huge crystals are made perfect in complete isolation from any sort of vibrational interference. They were slowly grown deep inside the tunnels of the continent. Their size dwarfed anything we had learned to make before. They were no less than 6 leagues(36 feet) in diameter, nearly a hundred times larger than when the Aleons were here. The Taoi field will be our crowning glory, our supreme accomplishment, as a tribute to those who came from the stars one day. They will truly make Atlantis the greatest and the most powerful empire the world has ever known.

When the Taoi are exposed to the One, their combined energy will create a field that will engulf the entire continent with unlimited power, to do with whatever we want and desire. As wonderful as that sounded, the idea of that kind of power, without the wisdom to manage it, offered only an ill feeling, a foreboding and many sleepless nights filled with worry for the King.

The younger members of the High Council secretly conferred with certain Baal Engineers and the infamous Galmutin, who resided quietly within the Baal clan. They secretly planned and conspired a new purpose for the Taoi field, conceived and developed as an adaptation and use of the energy utilized to accelerate mental functioning aboard the Antares.

Their concept could not be achieved without tremendous energy, the kind and level of energy that was in that engine room. The Taoi field, soon to be erected, will be used to increase another kind of power, only recently discovered by the Baal, a psychic power believed to be an even greater achievement. The young lords would not stop with a mere increase in their mental acuity, their ambitions would raise their energy to the greatest level, the level of the gods themselves.

While this nefarious activity went on, there was the problem of the remaining altered women, who lived just outside the City of the Realm. Their presence was embarrassing. They were rejected as misfits. As neither Aleon or Atlantean, just hybrids considered as rejects of the gods.

The unanimous decision to drive them from the Atlantean lands and beyond, a society in love with creating their own beauty, cursed to escape Atlantis into the hinterlands to the North. They settled in the icy regions, eventually creating their own civilization, the Anem people of Hyperborea.

Our understanding of Natural Forces expanded into vast amounts of knowledge. It soon became clear, the record keepers' ways of storing that knowledge completely overwhelmed the adequacy of the old ways.

In the earlier period of Atlantean history, we developed a system of writing down our language. The style of the language was a cuneiform pattern of symbols where each symbol contained not just a singular letter relating to an alphabet. Whole concepts could be implied just by adding a few different strokes.

The scribes would go to the river beds, at the base of Scartera, gather the volcanic soil as mud, form it into plates then let the plates dry until slightly hard, then imprint those cuneiforms with beveled wooden sticks. The plates were baked in the light of the One into hard stone-like tablets designed to permanently preserve those writings.

Changes in our knowledge came so rapidly, almost daily. The scientists intuited a better way to record events. Instead of using beveled sticks, we burned images and writing onto plates made of thin crystal grown in our laboratories, using light beams generated by the small crystal generators we originally used for heat and light in the cities and homes.

Even that process grew tiresome and inadequate. Continuing to find more dynamic ways to illustrate our thoughts, we discovered that our language and ideas could be stored into more than two dimensions within a single plate.

We found a way to energize the sublayers of a single crystal sheet, organizing the information at different angles using light combined with sound. Sound waves move in circles, so the original rectangular tablets did not favor the sound waves. Later, we used circular plates of crystal adapting well to the organizing sound patterns.

Each layer would have a different but harmonic frequency. By adjusting the angle of the light and frequency of sound embedded on each layer, placing each layer stacked on top of the layer below, shifting the viewing angle of the disc presented different images and writing. This afforded us to store a great deal more information on a single disc. By turning the disc, slight differences in perspective of the same image could also be seen.

We wanted to create dynamic, or moving illustrations while retaining the writing content in our spoken language. We realized that if we then placed the circular plates stacked together, with some method to cause the stacked circular plates to spin on the edge of the circular plates, we could create moving images and sound without manually turning them by hand. The speed of turning the discs exceeded the ability to turn the discs by hand. Then we created a method of turning the discs automatically.

Using the inherent electricals built up between the layers of a single disc, we realized we could use the cold magnetic force generated below the surface the plates rested on, to interact with the plates causing them to spin continuously. Once the turning was initiated by one who wanted to view and listen, the cold magnetic force balanced the discs while providing the motive force to turn them.

By adjusting the varying intensity of the cold magnetic force below, we could also adjust the rotational speed of the disc. Thus, we built large rooms with many such magnetic surfaces. Against the inside walls of these rooms held thousands of such discs. Ultimately, these rooms became our vast library of knowledge where people could come and watch, listen and learn at their leisure.

The laborious burning of still images onto discs became a problem and retarded our desire to record events in real time. The engineers found a way to make spinning wheels with many discs mounted on the surface, while a light beam generated inside a machine would mix with the light and sounds coming from outside.

This action allowed machines to dynamically record real action with light and sound. The reverse process would allow someone at a remote place, to playback the recorded images on a similar machine. To provide that feature to all places in Atlantis, the engineers simply added the stream to the Taoi, transmitting them to playback machines everywhere. This became our primary way of communicating to the people in the latter days.

A peculiar effect from watching these images and sounds coming from the playback machines, caused concern in the medical facilities. Analyzing the effects with test subjects, odd responses within the viewer's body, in particular, with the organs inside their bodies, caused changes within their DNA when certain patterns were seen and heard. This discovery became a keen interest of Galmutin. He set up a special team of engineers to explore this effect to better understand the interaction of the light and sound patterns upon these special organs.

Certain enzymes and hormonal fluids responsible for genetic changes ascertained and utilized by the outworlders, in their re-education and intellectual improvement process, provided insight for Galmutin's crew of engineers.

Galmutin encouraged them to learn how to augment this process of genetic changing to go far beyond the purposes the outworlders had conceived. Galmutin now had a way to increase the development of psychic abilities, enhancing both physical strength, mental abilities and psychic powers providing recipients with god like qualities.

Galmutin possessed one more chance to worm his way back into the High Council's graces.

He sought to tempt the ambition of the young lord governors with ultimate power. He came out of hiding, sending an envoy of Baal scientists to beseech the audience of the High Council, and requested a special meeting to present their findings.

Raag, the King, immediately declined his offer. His veto was ultimately overturned by the Council. Without choice, Raag reluctantly submitted to the presentation offered.

Senior members of the Council protested this obvious misuse of the Techlogi.

Heated arguments for and against the use of this procedure went on for days. Finally, out of the six Regional Governors, four of the six agreed, while two declined, including the King. The four represented the youngest of the governors.

Galmutin left the citadel smiling with glee. His plan included some of the governors, but he secretly had the engineers construct the new machine with some patterns that would cause the advanced changes while other patterns used would only offer minor changes. Of course, he argued that his new machine would be used on the

Council members only, while excluding the general populus until later.

He would secretly use the real patterns on himself and two of the governors, he trusted to stand beside him. His ultimate goal, replacing Raag on the throne.

Meanwhile, Galmutin realized that once on the throne, he would not be able to trust the Tec warriors to support his usurping Raag as supreme leader of Atlantis.

Using his new adaptive Techlogi, he began to experiment combining attributes of other species possessing some of the properties he wanted in his future army. Many experiments failed to merge effectively with the DNA of his Atlantean subjects. In order to protect the secrecy of his experiments including his disastrous failures, he kept his test subjects imprisoned.

Then the colonies of ants nearby inspired further study of their behavioral attributes. The ants (called anthropids), were gigantic during our time, reaching almost a foot in length, and being carnivores, they were dangerous in their own right. It was wise to steer clear of their colonies.

If Galmutin could successfully merge the Anthropid's DNA, they would be perfect super soldiers to do his bidding. Many months went by trying to adjust his adaptive machine to work with the DNA of the Anthropids. Galmutin refused to give up on his pet project, being an essential part of his plan to seize control of the City of the Realm and take the throne.

Then one day he succeeded. One of his test subjects' left fore arm began to change. First the fingers retracted, wilting to become monstrous three toed claws.

The thorax of his test subject became enlarged while the pelvic region shrank. Soon the subject legs became exaggeratedly muscular leaving joints quite lean.

Finally, the neck of the subject reduced to barely covering an enlarged skeletal structure supporting a bifurcated cranium, also enlarged were the eye sockets and the eyes were dissolved into massive multifaceted ocular domes. The subject lost the power of speech but seemed to respond to simple commands. His new soldier was complete. Now to determine how this 9-foot tall monster could be multiplied into an army worthy of his command.

Galmutin realized that a general, commanding an army ground assault, could perhaps be confronted by the Realm's Tec troops wielding light weapons and be overtaken. The Anthropid's three toed claws made it impossible to handle a light weapon. He needed a new weapon that could take out thousands of Tec troops in one sweeping motion. He pondered to remove a Taoi from one of the temples and modify its purpose, but that would be discovered immediately, destroying the Atlantean source of power, the same power that provided the underpinning of his laboratory experiments.

So, he conceived of his own Taoi, built and modified as a powerful weapon that would stand at the front lines of his offense. This would offset his plans for the near future, but he was willing to wait for assured victory. He needed time to amass his army of Anthropids in any case.

The growth and construction of a Taoi weapon would take a minimum of two cycles of the One. The problem of keeping that activity a secret was troublesome.

Galmutin thought.

'Well… I could train several engineers, then get rid of them when it's finished, a bit messy but I can deal with that later.

***

The King gave Yokar freedom to leave his post as Regent Council for the evening. The priest entered the Temple of Knowledge to meditate on the ominous feeling he experienced over the previous few days. He was not sure if it be an omen or not. So, he entered the cave of the unknown, a volcanic stone structure with a domed roof, lined with Auriculum, and inside a copper geometric, as a three-sided pyramid frame, surrounded the central space.

While inside, he went into deep levels of consciousness. His mind flashed many images lingering, sometimes overlapping and dissolving from one to the other.

Suddenly, he saw Galmutin laughing. Then his mind wandered into blackness a little until, a vision of a Taoi loomed into view. He noticed that it wasn't finished. He opened his eyes with a euphony. I must seek out Galmutin and learn of his nefarious plans.

On the morning of the next day, Yokar entered the Citadel. He made his way into the throne room to speak with King Raag.

"Sire…in my meditation last night, I had a vision, it seemed somehow prophetic, yet that is not one of my gifts."

The King turned from what he was looking at with some surprise and curiosity.

"So…Raag said with a chuckle…shall I change your title from Counsel to Prophet then?"

"No…Sire…I believe my best talents are to counsel the King on all affaires pertaining to concerns of the throne."

Raag replied.

"Well…yes you are right of course…who would I choose to replace my best Counsel? So… he went on…tell me of your news, my friend."

"Yes sire…Yokar continued…I saw Galmutin, he was laughing…but that was not all. The very next vision was a Taoi, a large one similar to the temples on the mountain tops. I thought that perhaps there is a connection. I cannot wonder why a Taoi would be needed. The system is balanced and could not, by adding a fourth crystal improve the field." I experienced great sadness and concern with this vision, it spells great calamity, I am sure of it…Sire."

The King declared.

"Well we cannot afford to dismiss the visions of a King's Counselor. He turned and ordered his court adjutants to post more Tec guards at the temples. It occurs to me, we have not seen the likes of Galmutin for a long time. Only to argue for the applications of Techlogi in the Council meeting.

The Tehlon Clan, also known as the overseers, kept much of their work in the Temple of Knowledge secret. When Raag, King of Atlantis, chose Yokar as his Regent Counselor, he would have many private meetings with the High Priest regarding the importance of the temple and its role in the furthering of the culture and understanding of Natural Forces. Unlike his father, King Tatsukin, who ruled the realm with a different focus.

The similarities between them centered around a love of the empire and the care of the inhabitants. Their differences, in some ways, quite stark and precise. Raag revered the many cultural and symbolic attitudes that were the foundation and underpinning of the civilization, the power of might establishing rightfulness was one such attitude, so battles for the supremacy of truth in action were fundamental.

Raag was a visionary, not in the same way as his father, who believed strongly that a prosperous culture meant making sure the infrastructure of the colony was maintained. Tatsukin was first a warrior, he believed in a strong defense. He encouraged the development of a formidable army of Tec warriors, well trained and efficient with fighting skills. With Lemuria and its diverse culture as the primary adversary, that defense was needed in the event of a possible attack, moreover, a general maintenance of civil order within all of the clans during peaceful times became a first priority.

Making sure the grain coffers were full, in the event of changing weather patterns, the exchange of goods and services between clans flowed without difficulty, as another primary goal.

Raag came into rulership with much of those concerns already well established and any civil disturbances were nothing more than minor instances and easily handled with wise action.

Raag, through his influence and relationship with Yokar, focused more on the inner life of the inhabitants, the preservation of knowledge and spiritual development. Until the time of his rule, there was only the Temple of Power and the Temple of Beauty, which included the health and wellbeing on a physical level, centered around the the baths of Malagra on the Isle of Tiber, near what is now Bimini in the Bahamas. This temple possessed great healing spas of Sulphur impregnated warm seawaters and healing centers utilizing the powers of light, color and sound.

The Temple of Power, devoted to the development and control of Natural Forces, was the first and only temple in Atlantis. With the Temple of Power, devoted to the Law of One, and the original Law Givers, Kantsu and Tiantsu.

Through their many consultations, Raag and Yokar considered that a life of toil without meaning was a travesty. Through Yokar's powers of intuition and mental skills of meditation and communications with the gods of higher consciousness, a system of development, based upon the understanding of Natural Forces as they related to the functioning of those forces within the body and the mind, became the cornerstone of the temple. Many techniques and practices were established in tiers of learning within a priest's experience, until a level of advancement could be achieved.

Only men were allowed to enter the Temple of Knowledge, a rudimentary axiom that men were the most important of the male and female familial constant. Women always found their way in the support of the male.

Children conceived were mere chattel and unimportant in their early development, males were then separated from the females and treated quite differently. The role of females did not include learning the basic arts of battle, only in basic ways for self-defense.

Yokar explained to Raag.

"To create balance in the external Natural Forces, a certain understanding of the Center of Balance was needed to be recognized and acknowledged within one's consciousness inside. The concept of the Neutral Force (Perutii Rogalin) was a fundamental axiom in the training.

Yokar proposed:

"A fulcrum over a set of wheels on a common axel, to define the center of polarity between the backward pull and forward pull around the center, the center of the two forces form the Neutral Point. This Neutral Point could be discovered by trial and error, internally, by utilizing the inner sensitivity of the Neutral Point of the fulcrum within the consciousness.

"The knowledge of the marked division of the polarizing forces could be used with an advantage, to pose one force over the other in a controlled way by unbalancing the Neutral Point one way or the other. Taking a two wheeled cart carrying a load effected by the cold magnetic force pulling the cart to the earth, what we call gravity, the force could be used to pull the cart forward or backward instead of adding the brute action of a third force provided by an animal to overcome the primary force of 'gravity' keeping it stationary. Then, with only the slight application of an upper force to manage the Neutral Point just beyond imbalance, the cart would be driven by gravity instead of using the added third force. This was the underlying principle behind all of the Techlogi used in Atlantis.

Another example of temple training was with the use of shape. Yokar continued.

"There is the use of shape, but to do this, a different way of perceiving reality is needed. Normally, an individual would perceive items and actions around them in a singular fashion, meaning each would be seen as separate entities in a series or string. But if all the items or actions could be embraced at once, that impression would constitute a three-dimensional form, and that form would be the shape of all of the items or actions put together. The form of that shape defines a hidden aspect of reality that would normally be illusive to the perceiver. Then the form is a positive mold that behaves like a stamp on the mind. If then the stamp would be the positive polarity, or problem to be solved, what then would the negative hollow mold represent? It would become its polar opposite; the negative form would then become the solution once realized as the Neutral Center. Like adding the brute third force to the cart, the energy used to solve the problem would take more effort than necessary.

"By simply allowing the negative form to make an impression allowes the mind to take advantage of the unseen component of reality. The unseen component of the mind is intuition and the unbalancing of the Neutral Force releases the solution without any effort. This is what you might call a euphony.

Other practices within the temple training included something called the 'Dragon's Breath'.

This practice consists of deep rapid breathing along with physical movements of dynamic and static actions reflecting again the polarizing forces Agogik or positive force and Magogik or negative force vs. the Neutral Force or Peruitii Rogalan internally.

Yokar explained.

"In order for the deepening and expanding of consciousness to occur, a pattern of combined action must be actualized with the body. The aspirant would stand over a point where the earth force is abundant emerging through the floor of the temple.

"Standing as if straddled sitting on a Quanah, deep rapid breaths would begin for at least twenty repetitions with the last breath expelled creating a vacuum, using Polar Forces, and then Neutral component of the Earth Force comes within the body starting at the bottom of the spinal column, it wriggles as it rises and feels just like a Barthis worm writhing on the end of a fishing pole. This is done in a series of 4 positions that accentuate the

Earth force entering other parts of the body including the limbs and upper thorax.

"The aspirant begins stomping around with bare feet on the temple floor, while smacking the occipital region of the head with both hands.

Finally, the aspirant stands again in the 'sitting position upon a Quanah', shaking the head from side to side, while throat singing in two octaves, one lower and one upper. This process is repeated for 9 levels, each level would require the passage of increasing repititions exponentially.

Yokar continued.

"The next exercise is related to the use of Silent Vril, a spiritual language brought to the Temple by the gods. This was called the Taumlec Arc. A set of Jub jub nutshells strung together to allow the precise counting of 60 counts at each of the four quadrants (a total of 240 counts is considered one Arc). The Vril sounds spoken silently, were accompanied by visualized colors in the four quadrants, blue at the groin, red like the color of the lava of Scartera on the right shoulder, green as the color of the Popul tree leaves on the left shoulder, and finally, white as the color of ice on top of Palinor, at the crown of the head. All of these positions were accompanied by four Vril expressions as each pattern of expression spoken silently for 60 counts: ONJNG; RAT-RUSE; KPT-HAN; AUM-HAN respectively. This was done for thirty Arcs, lasting more than 18 hours at one sitting.

Yokar Continued on.

"Then another exercise involves visualizing a flattened triangle, within the mind, with a golden color similar to the setting orb of the One. Then, while focusing the attention inside the triangle, listening to the heart beating while imagining two orbs on each end of the triangle's base pulsing on and off alternately with the rhythms of the heart. This gave the power of the long sight, or clairvoyance, for viewing the past or the future."

Yokar concluded.

"The last set of exercises relate to something called the Torax. This practice involved the application of sexual energy mixed with feelings and stored within three-sided pyramid forms merging with two four-sided pyramids and spun clockwise and counter clockwise around the heart.

"Based upon the wisdom of Kantsu and Tiantsu, the ability to alter the shape of the Heart Pukka for higher spiritual development, relates to the problem of the three knots of the Heart Puuka, (a Puuka is a window - different from the Indo-Ayran chakra) relating to pride, fear and greed. The knots keep these negative forces from being released because they are bound like a knot with sexual energy. To untie the knots, pure elements, combined with geometric forms are then spun clockwise and counter-clockwise, again applying the Neutralizing Force to the Heart Puuka.

"Two 4-sided pyramids are visualized, one inverted just above the Heart Puuka with its apex facing the lower 4-sided pyramid below the heart Puuka. Both having 3-sided pyramids containing the stored feelings and the sexual energy all positioned at the four corners of each 4-sided pyramid. These are both rotated in opposite directions and eventually, will merge to form a dodecahedron shape at the center of the Heart Puuka. This is done to neutralize all knots completely.

"Our system of spiritual development in the Temple of Knowledge is based and dependent on the balance of all the Puukas. Puukas are windows of awareness with the shape of the soul at each dimensional level, from the groin to the crown. It's not important that the energy of each Puuka is strong or weak, present or vacant. All Puukas are open all the time, but the balance of their energies flowing from one to another, is the most significant in your training.

"Raag…to make the most effective use of your talents and skills, to make your rulership count as the most significant ruler in the City of the Realm, you need to complete your temple training. Unlike your father, who had no interest in such matters, you will become the greatest ruler for all time."

Raag replied.

"Master Yokar…will all of this training take very long?"

Yokar replied.

"Do not concern yourself with the time it takes to master the training. All of the training has but one requirement…You must have a burning desire."

Raag said.

"Master Yokar…what do you mean by a burning desire?"

Yokar smiled and answered.

"Imagine… I would take you in a boat out to the inlet sea. There I would ask you to step out of the boat. Then, I would grasp your lock of hair and plunge you below the surface for a considerable time. And after that time, I would pull you from the sea and ask you one question: 'what was the most significant and important thought that first entered your mind?' You would say… 'all I want to do is take a breath!'…and that my young friend is…a burning desire!"

Galmutin rushed to provide additional advancements, promised to the young lords on the Council. He was not being careful about every aspect of the side effects of these changes to their DNA and their nervous system.

He focused on the endocrine system and the nerve plexus along the spinal cord.

The engineers did not realize the implications of increasing the desirable attributes, unaware of the dangers of going too far, too quickly. They did not consider the impact of these changes on the psychological makeup and mental stability.

When Captain Adalon explained the re-education process to Raag, he mentioned briefly, how precise the changes needed to be and the importance of gradual induction, in order to protect the integrity of mental stability and the personality profile.

In the same way, his experiments with merging ant consciousness and physical attributes to an Atlantean body were also overlooked. His ambition and impatience overwhelmed his diligence to follow a reasonable approach.

Many Atlantean subjects died almost

immediately in the earlier experiments. He kept those that survived in holding cells while the failed rejected bodies, burned in an open pit.

In time, he could maintain a modicum of physical stability, but the life span of the new Anthropid creature would last only a few days before the process would begin to revert. At the same time, vital signs entered into catastrophic collapse ending in their death.

Galmutin became irritable and scolded his engineers often, complaining of their inabilities to accomplish his goals, in the time allotted. They fell short of his expectations.

He still had not solved the problem of life span, while at the same time, the problem of replicating his Anthropids posed a conundrum. If he made changes in their reproduction elements, he risked their reproduction to become rampant and out of his control. He preferred to utilize and apply Atlantean concepts of selective breeding.

He could not reconcile an ant in its original form, multiplied by the virtue of a viral reproduction process, that had nothing to do with birthing vs. conception. He was working with a fundamentally beast-like lifeform. So, applying Atlantean concepts was not going to work. He intuited that the life span problem could be related to the replication question.

He told his engineers to begin focusing on the viral nature of the ant reproduction process, perhaps in that, he could develop a way to extend the life span, but then purposefully offering, the Anthropid a predetermined life span, thus limiting its ability to reproduce in an unlimited way. This idea provided some comfort in knowing that if anything should go badly, the limited lifespan would be an innate failsafe to his creation.

In his Anthropid experiments, he failed to notice the creature's proclivity toward unprovoked violence erupting unexpectedly and with pronounced increase. He didn't think the new adaptive machine would ultimately bring dynamic changes to Atlantean subjects also, including aberrant mental behavior and pronounced violent responses.

Council meetings continued without incident at first. Then over time, Raag and Yokar noticed a distinct change in the attitudes of the younger regional governors. Outbursts of unwarranted rage became the norm during meetings. At times, Raag would have to interrupt meetings, delay continued discussion for another time just to ensure the rage did not become violent, with one governor attacking another without provocation.

Some of the governors met secretly with Galmutin in a clandestine location to vent their frustrations. They were also impatient and had greater expectations regarding significant improvements with their mental acuity as well as, promised increases in strength and this mysterious psychic ability Galmutin professed.

He tried to quell their impatience with reason, explaining that he did not want to endanger their existing properties already achieved by the re-education machine from the Antares craft. He dared not reveal the difficulties he experienced in his laboratory, for fear they would learn of his failures and reject his efforts.

At the same time, progress of the creation of another Taoi suffered many setbacks as well. There were unforeseen impurities in the chemical makeup of the growing bath. The seed crystal would develop fissures at earlier stages of growth, making the Taoi unstable if and when power was stored and then drawn out in the death ray of light strong enough to cause great destruction at anything it was aimed at.

The engineers considered many areas where problems with the bath, the magnetic cold force applied and the chemical composition of the bath itself were analyzed. All these investigations consumed months of time and effort delaying positive results, building new frustrations which Galmutin could not contain. He also used the new Adaptive Machine for accelerated DNA development on himself, confident that he could keep one step ahead of his fellow governors in the process.

His rising aggression and changes in temperament escaped his notice. His anger and frustration seemed appropriate, while he chastised his underperforming engineering crew.

Now he had lost all independent prospective, regarding all his plans, making him even more maniacal, while he continued to make unreasonable demands.

With the conditions of the growing bath for the Taoi improved and the stability of the cold magnetic force generator stabilized, a new seed was introduced. Unfortunately, a new wrinkle developed for the first time. The tunnels bored into the earth below mount Scartera, where the secret bath was located, were violently shaken by an earthquake. Parts of the tunnel collapsed and the unexpected violent shaking disturbed the seed crystal and the whole process had to be redone. Now the building of the Taoi could not begin until a new bath facility could be constructed.

Fear of another shaking of the ground, convinced the engineers to begin digging a new bore hole at the base of Palinor. This location posed logistical problems with transporting engineers, equipment and materials found only at the base of Scartera, the only volcanic mountain in Atlantis. In addition, cause for drilling a new bore hole at the foot of Palinor had to be justified with the High Council and the King Regent.

The engineering team came before the Council to explain their reasons for such activity. Their reasons were vague, but they explained falsely, that a new source of metallic materials were discovered in that location, so their drilling reflected an exploratory search only. The reasons given seemed plausible and no contest about their pursuit, was given. With that, many more months passed until a new bath site could be built at Palinor.

***

Galmutin determined that the innate property of the fertilization from a queen ant to produce the first workers, created an inherent 4-5-day limit in the lifespan of the worker. This became his next focal point. Some way of identifying this genetic predisposition offered from the queen, to the newly emerging egg pupa, led Galmutin to examine the genetic profile of the queen. He needed to determine when and how this transmigration of genetic code could be altered or eliminated.

Also, he realized the reproductive scheme nature created within the ant colony and the queen's role, was incredibly significant. A new confidence arose within Galmutin and his mood changed.

News of a minor aftershock at Scartera brought fear of another major setback. The engineers conferred with Galmutin and assured him with the new location of Palinor, the aftershock was negligible, having little or no effect on the stability of the new bath apparatus. They confirmed the new location was ideally suited for their work, and they believed the new Taoi would be ready with the newly adjusted time frame Galmutin established.

At the Citadel, one of the young Regional Governors requested a cup of fermented scawberry before the Council meeting was to begin. The Council adjutant placed the cup in front of the governor and when he reached for the cup, it moved slightly beyond his reach! This action startled him for the moment. The adjutant stared at the cup for a moment, then dismissed what he saw as a mistake in perception. The governor dismissed the phenomenon as his clumsiness to push the cup away.

There were other incidents with the other governors as well. Various abilities appearing spontaneously indicated that Galmutin's new Adaptive Machine was showing results.

***

The dwarf star, twin to the One, emerged in its orbit at perihelion, swinging through the existing solar system of the One with 7 of its own planets. This orbital path, the gazers noticed, would cycle every 3600 years.

The star gazers of the Tasher Clan watched with horror as the dwarf star passed through the night sky like a great and terrible comet. This was the first of many dark omens for the Atlantean culture. After the Dwarf star, the brother God Alta, passed the One, caused many earthquakes to occur in the land. Scartera responded with a series of eruptions.

These events spelled doom for our world. The Gods were angry, especially the Brother God Alta. These emergencies created panic for all inhabitants of the Realm. They ran to the Citadel crying out to challenge the King to do something.

Raag ordered all inhabitants to escape to the mountainous regions of the continent. While the approach to Earth of the god Alta (dwarf star) was close, Alta brought with it more horror. One of the planets orbiting Alta clipped the second moon Raika, causing that moon to explode and fall out of orbit around earth.

Large fragments broke away into space, but the main fragment of the moon descended into the western seas, destroying the continent of Gwandana. All of Lemuria plunged into the sea in just a few days. Afterward, only islands remained, now known as; the Solomons of Oceana, including islands in the south, New Guinea, Tuvalu, Vanuatu, Australia, Madagascar, and islands to the west and north, Hawaii, Japans, New Hebrides, Easter Island, Guam and the Philippines.

The resultant tidal waves washed over the Atlantean continent to the west and ingulfed many villages reaching to the foot of Scartera, Sepulva and Palinor. The tunnels bored into Palinor and the bath facility for the new Taoi were destroyed. Also, the Laboratory containing the five Anthropids, destroyed and the Anthropids all drowned.

It would be many years before the situation resembled normal life in Atlantis. All of Galmutin's plans disrupted once again. Fear from the wrath of the gods created chaos among the people and ruling for the Realm became even more difficult. This prompted a strategic plan for new rulership to form more quickly among the young governors.

During Council meetings arguments regarding the failure of Raag to negotiate a peace with the gods irrupted quite often. Even the Regent Counsel experienced greater difficulty to maintain control inside the Council room and among the people. Yokar warned Raag that there was great unrest among the people of all the clans.

One day Yokar pulled Raag aside to offer some suggestions.

"Sire…perhaps it would be good to offer the people who have been the most effected by the recent calamities, a sanctioned reconstruction of their villages. Supply them with additional provisions of fresh food and water, even ample supplies of fermented Scawberry to easy their pain when they visit bistros to forget their troubles. I believe this approach will help to engender a softer perspective about their King."

Raag replied.

"I understand and greet your shape with positive acknowledgement, I am concerned that even the coffers of the citadel, run thin and we did not want to eliminate those supplies, in the event that more catastrophes have been planned by the angry gods…But I will consider your suggestions with gratitude."

Yokar replied.

"Sire…you remember my visions? …I have discovered the remains of an unbuilt Taoi at the foot of Palinor. Not to worry, the land quakes and water floods have destroyed Galmutin's efforts for now. Also, I found the remains of some very strange creatures floating in the tidal waters. I cannot imagine how they came to be? They have never before been seen in this land, unless they have emerged from the tunnels and released from the land quakes.

"I believe your primary concern is to thwart growing support for the young governors, they are now your primary risk to your continued rule.

The Council's attitude toward exploration of new lands beyond the continent became the basis for more conflict. The elder governors ruled against anything beyond the old ways of separatism viewing the use of airships for nothing more than discovery of new raw materials.

The young governors struggled to hide their rapidly advancing abilities of clairvoyance and telekinesis, while they openly used their power to reach into another's mind. Their strength also increased. Though their bodies didn't change in size, their musculature settled with stronger denser bones, tougher skin and courser hair.

After a heated debate, the Council was adjourned for a short time while King Raag spoke privately with his Regent Counselor, Yokar.

"Yokar…you have been more than a Counsel to the throne, you have been my closest friend and ally. I wanted to talk about the younger governors. They seem markedly different in the last few months. They are more aggressive, their attitude towards the throne borders on disrespect and sometimes challenging. Their overly confident posturing reaches suspect of my authority as King."

Yokar replied.

"Yes…Sire…I have noticed it too. They seem to be a separated group, their shape is quite different, beyond what would normally be related to their youthful lack of wisdom and recklessness.

I suspect they have done something to change their condition. I will pursue this Sire and confer my findings to you as soon as I know something of substance."

Raag continued.

"Actually, there is something else. I felt a feeling I have not felt in several hundreds of years, a fear for my life. I wonder if these governors are plotting against me, to threaten my life, to seize the throne by force"

Yokar responded compassionately.

" Hmmm…he grunted. Yes…it would follow, these aberrant changes would suggest a possible insurrection ending in a vile act of that sort.

"I will order more Tec guards to the Citadel, in particular the throne chamber.

This will deter any shadow conspiracy toward that end."

Raag continued.

"Yes…of course that is prudent my friend, but how do we know the influence remains within their midst. How do we know for sure we can trust the Tec to defend the throne? After all, even though Shirac is an elder member and Regional Governor of the Tec clan, his disagreement of my policies, have been rising more frequently recently. It's as though the younger members are adversely affecting him."

Yokar listened to his King carefully, noting his rising paranoia. Then added.

"Yes, I have noticed this as well, however, please consider that Shirac as well as Telas, who is also an elder, disagrees with the advancing Techlogi throughout the Realm. He is also in disagreement with the use of exploration as an excuse to broaden the realm to the shores of other lands."

"Perhaps they do not challenge your authority but grumble about the influx of Techlogi disrupting the old ways, fearing a threat of anger with the One."

Raag relaxed to the sound of Yokar's answer. He then declared the Council meeting to reconvene. All members re-entered the Council Chamber and sat at their respective positions. The young governors immediately re-entered the discussion about exploration and expansion.

Governor Taric, Galmutin's replacement, began.

"There has been much talk about keeping to ourselves. The expansion into other lands is for replenishment of our resources only. But I disagree. The people of other lands are below our level of civilization and deserved to be conquered. Do you really believe they would not pose a threat to the empire?"

Grumbling and side discussion of his remarks erupted. Yokar had to pound his staff to the floor of the chamber to bring about order.

Telas responded.

"I believe our expansion into other lands is a gesture of good will and will engender a response of goodwill from the other outer tribes."

Taric responded.

"Telas you are blinded by your excitement with new buildings to make. You cloak your shape of ambition to show off your skills as architect of the Realm. We have been to the hinterlands with our surveys. I tell you… those other outer tribes you speak of so highly, are primitive, nothing more than the beasts that roam our lands. Would you approach a Quanah with such elevated exchange, of course not! Your argument has no merit!"

Telas defended.

"Would it not be in alignment with the old ways of the Law Givers, Kantsu and Tiantsu, that sharing our advanced knowledge with those who could make use of it would encourage those tribes to share the wealth of their natural resources easily, without conflict?"

Taric replied with anger.

"The old ways are filled with weakness and lack vision. What about the old way of Battle? … to win battles, is a cleaner, truer way…fighting defines what is right and rightfully the spoils of battle go to the winner."

Taric continued in his tirade.

"We have the means of flight, we have the high ground for battle. We also have Mash-Mak (fire rays), hand weapons of the One. That means the One wants us to enter into other lands by force and take what is ours."

There was an instant response to Taric's apparent rekindling of the joy and pleasure of battle, erupting in cheers and clapping for his statements.

Taric went on.

"I believe we should build smaller Taoi, mount them aboard our airships and descend upon our enemies in those other lands with glory and vengeance! They will come to know us with fear and trepidation, they will come to know us as their gods, gods of fire from the sky."

The younger governors pounded on the Council table in a frenzy of rebel rousing excitement. A vote to build an armada of airships loaded with Mash-Mak weapons, was cast and all but one declined, the King.

With a year of the One passing, the airships were completed. The smaller Taoi, grown to become Mash-Mak weapons, mounted aboard. Three warriors sat in the craft, one to navigate, one to pilot and one to handle the Mash-Mak weapon. On board, in the engine room contained a secondary crystal stored with enough energy to carry them aloft and to go beyond the nightside veil of energy normally supplying the power to move about over the Atlantean continent.

Taric would be the lead ship commander, a ship designed for 4 occupants. The occupants were made of Tec warriors. They set out to go beyond the southern seas to a land sounth of Gwandana, a region known as Mazatland (Now called Central America) . As they reached its shores, the lay of the land was flat and covered with dense jungle. There were no signs of organized living, no cities, no villages visible.

The crews of the aerial craft were unaware that the natives of this land observed the craft with wonder, watching them beneath the wide leaves of wild banana trees. These natives were the forerunners of the Mayan and Aztec tribes, the Toltec, Olmec, and Zapotec of what is now central and south America.

After witnessing the Sky Gods appearing overhead, they began to build pyramids rising well above the local terrain like the one at Chichen Itza to observe them more closely. The Gods didn't return however. They continued to move south along what would later become the Yucatan peninsula then toward South America. They discovered high in the Andean summits, another primitive culture called the Mochica Indians.

The armada returned to Atlantis with news of the far lands, and the promise of building fortifications in those places offering strategic outposts of the empire. Later they were to return to these places wiping out entire colonies of natives leaving no trace of their assault. The Yucatan was deemed to have no military advantage being part of the lowlands. On the Andean peak, of what is now Machu Piccu, Atlantean airships landed along with builders and architects from the Yaga Clan.

They used the airship mash-Mak weapons to heat the surface of rocks, making their surfaces soft and plasma-like. Borrowing from their airships motive power, the nightside of the cold magnetic Natural Forces, provided a way to lift and slide the rocks together, to form seamless fortifications, suitable to defend the mountain should the need arise.

They did not leave anyone to man the fortifications after they wiped out the Mochica tribes, indigenous to the area. Instead, they needed to return to the motherland, utilizing the remaining reserves of power from the onboard crystals.

Now Taric could return triumphant, having established outposts to expand the empire and at the same time, conquering the enemies of the Realm.

Upon Taric's return, Raag challenged him in the courtyard of the Citadel.

"So, you arrive in a charade of a hero's welcome, but what of your exploits, where are your enemy captives to prove your conquests?"

Taric replied with a sardonic smile.

"Oh… a small matter really… we simply vaporized the enemy with our superior weapons of Mash-Mak. They were no match for our Atlantean forces. If there were any survivors, I'm sure they scattered to the four winds of the God Tyree."

Raag continued to argue.

"So, you show no courage of hand to hand battle! You stand apart and devastate at a safe distance, where is the honor in that, Young Hero?" Taric replied grumbling.

"Raag…you are King, but you lead our world with a weak hand, still believing in the old antiqu- ated beliefs of our forefathers, the Law Givers. I tell you, I believe your time of leadership is passing, as is your vitality, you are not getting any younger! A day will come when new leadership is in order!"

With that remark, Taric left the Citadel feeling as though he had the last word.

***

Taric and the other young lords, Shirac, Baalene and Paader gathered at the laboratory to speak with Galmutin about their progress. Galmutin was eager to share with them his progress.

"We are close my friends to realizing our dream, the supreme rulership of the Realm. Now, along with the outposts you have gathered under the Realm's possessions, the Realm will govern even the unknown worlds with awesome power.

Soon, Raag and his band of weaklings will be gone. Then, I, Galmutin along with my trusted staff, my adjutant generals, shall rule with a stronger hand over this mighty Realm.

In a fortnight, the Taoi will be ready for the assault on the City of the Realm.

All cheered to the sound of that news, all except Taric. He harbored jealousy and rebuke of Galmutin's claim to the throne. He believed he

should become the King as reward for his brave and bold pursuits of expanding the Realm and conquering all of the enemies of Atlantis. He kept silent. He waited for the right moment where he could assassinate Galmutin and rise to the rightful place of King. He strongly
believed he would have the strong support of the other Regional Governors and the Tec warriors.

In that moment Galmutin revealed the other news. The news of the creation of his new warriors, the Anthropids. He called one forth and they were shocked at the sight of this new creation of his. As the Anthropid stood motionless within the group, they walked around the beast, both admiring its massive body and claws. They felt a shudder of terror and horror by its overall menacing appearance.

Galmutin standing in front of the beast declared.

"Well…what do you think of my new soldier?"

The governors were almost speechless, still gawking at the monster.

Then Baaleen spoke.

"Are you sure about this monstrous creation of

yours? …I mean how on earth did you create such a thing? …Can it be trusted to follow orders?"

Galmutin replied.

"In most respects the creature is a worker slave, bred by his counterpart, the ant. You see… Galmutin added…The ant colony is made up of a queen and workers. Genetically speaking, they are perfect for their purpose. They are incredibly strong and not too bright, meaning they will follow orders easily. One drawback in the genetic makeup, their hands are claws, an unfortunate flaw I didn't count on. However, they will be the front line of offence backed up by the portable Taoi."

Taric replied.

"Okay now we have beasts at the front line, but how many of these did you create?"

Galmutin responded sheepishly.
"Well…in the moment, I only have five designed. I am still dealing with the problem of replication. But by the time they will be in play, I will have perhaps thousands."

Taric grunted in disbelief.

As the physical, mental and psychic abilities continued to increase among some of the Regional Governors, in particular, Patel of the Tehlon Clan, Agualar of the Faeylan clan and Falmot of the Saliene clan. Changes in their psychological and personality continued unchecked and became much more aggressive. Their physical appearance also altered significantly. Their skin began to take on a subtle glow which added to their excitement about becoming gods. These changes could not be hidden from others anymore, but no one dared to mention it.

The Council meetings became increasingly unruly with arguments rising each day. Little issues between clans had never been beyond mediation. Now, however, the issues arising, no matter how big or how small, were going well beyond mediation. Even Yokar could not contain their anger and resentment, which carried beyond the meetings and festered greater antagonisms even with the citizens.

Land quakes became frequent to the point of being a daily occurrence too. This made the situation more inflamed. Unspoken fears ran rampant among the people. They came to the court often speaking out that the King wasn't doing enough to protect them. Reactions to the earth shaking amongst the governors, as a whole, was summarily dismissed as minor events to the natural world. They spent time to coach the people not to worry, as these events wouldn't last long.

The King Raag expressed concern about this with Yokar.

"Yokar…what do you make of all this earth trembling?... the People are greatly stressed and demanding that I do something to fix the problem…I don't understand what's going on… How can I calm the people of the Realm when I am also disturbed by these events!"

Yokar replied.

"Yes Sire…I can appreciate your concern, both personally and politically. I have consulted the Tasher Clan…They tell me that there is much in the way of heavenly disturbance, small stars are falling to the earth more often. Strange appearances in the sky and altered weather may be another reaction to something approaching.

Mind you, the gazers do not know either. They

want to know what are the causes for these disturbances. I suggest that when you address the people, you refer to our conversations with the Tashers. It is suspected the luminaries in the night sky harbor anger and ill will toward the earth, something for which you cannot do anything about. Since it relates to the gods and their attitude, I suggest you tell them they should go to the temple, meditate and pray to the gods. In that way, they will feel useful and take more responsibility with their appeals."

Raag answered.

"Okay, I hear you counselor. And what is going on with the Regional Governors?

"I have heard talk amongst the Court Adjutants about rumors of civil war. I want to get ahead of that issue if possible. A civil war would be disastrous for the Realm."

Yokar acknowledged.

"Yes… My King, I have also heard of these rumors. I have not been able to determine their source however. I was not ready to bring it to your attention until I ascertained the validity of this seditious talk. If I learn of this, I will bring the issue and those responsible to you right away."

Raag replied.

"Very well, my friend. There is one other item I wanted to talk about…The Governor's seat for the Baal Clan is still vacant, since Adalon left. Galmutin has requested to be restored to that position. His argument mirrors the people of the Baal clan. They have no representation on the Council and I lean toward agreement. What do you think?"

Yokar paused to reply.

"Sire…it is your decision of course. Galmutin does pose a history of near seditionist ideals, suspecting he is jealous of you and has always questioned your right to rule…that alone brings concerns of his shape, to rule from that seat in a neutral way. My advice would be to allow it with the provision that he will be watched and scrutinized for his continued behavior, in the Council as well as, his fealty to the King."

Raag gave Yokar the sign of a warrior as he responded.

"Toshmalon Yokar, thank you for your continued support and wise counsel to the realm."

Yokar said, as he left the throne chamber.
"By your leave Sire."

***

Galmutin sat at his Manx(a chair and desk combined). The Manx perfectly adapts to the sitting person's body, in fact, the Manx could adapt to anyone's body, given only a few minutes exposure time.

He enjoyed the expansive feeling and the sense of personal power he experienced, during these last days, from the beginning of the treatment. The adjustment machine actually performed better than he expected. For him, the expanded awareness took second place to the impact of discovering his lust for more power, fundamental to his existence.

While he was contemplating that discovery, he suddenly met with a mysterious force that surrounded him, almost invisible. Only certain defined areas would show some reflective surfaces, defining a figure at times, which then could be detected.

Galmutin could feel a presence, palpable almost

to the touch. It would retreat if he reached out to touch the thing. In the midst of this experience, emerged a deep and hollow voice which, after moments, clearly spoke to him as it sat with him like a shadow, hanging around and over his head.

The voice said.

'Galmutin...you give me cause to come and observe who and what it is that has called upon me? ...For only being just a man, you possess much energy of the kind I'm looking for.

Galmutin paused in thought, of what was happening at that moment. *'He had crossed dimensions, entered the inner sanctum of the gods, including this god, who now reaches out to him.'*

Galmutin then said.

"And what is it you are looking for? You seem to think, I have it as well."

The voice again spoke.

'I am Beliel...I am the Lord Adjutant to Lucifer Morningstar of Aldebaran.

It is your anger, the strength of yourself(ego), also your pride and arrogance that interests me. Perhaps, it is good for both of us to work together for a common goal.

The presence of those underdeveloped creatures inhabiting your city is disgusting. Like vermin, they are below you and your greatness. You should rid them from your Realm. They will ultimately destroy your colony in time. I am here… to help you defeat those… who would belittle and challenge you.'

In that moment, the presence left him. Galmutin felt stunned, in awe about what he saw and felt. He considered, perhaps the machine had gone too far with him, his mind completely useless now. There was something else. He felt an urge to strike out at something, anything. The surge of energy continued to rise. He could hardly contain the power running through his body like a mighty river, washing away any doubt he might have held before.

He knew now, he must gather those who would follow him. Their divine purpose, to destroy the empire and raise the temples to the one true God… Beliel.

Beliel convinced Galmutin that the way of Techlogi was the one true way of the gods. If he were to rule, he would need to advance his culture with Techlogi first, then honor and worship Beliel, a god of Thunder and Lightning, who will raise him up as King of the entire empire and the rest of the world.

Lucifer Morningstar smiled in the shadows of Aldebaran. He boldly declared across the great quantum, *'man would of course, fall short. The great experiment will fail in Atlantis.'*

He said to Beliel.

'Make this place on the earth, the final battle ground of the fallen and unfallen.

'We will prove her way is wrong, we will not stop until the ways of The Law of One are distorted and destroyed, proving that earth, the remnant of the Most High's cherished world, Tiamat, shall never arise again.'

Beliel answered.

'Yes Sire...I will mold them in your image and usher in the way of your coming.'

***

Galmutin called a meeting with other members of the Council. The meeting, intended only for those supportive of an insurrection of the Realm, deposing Raag as King. Needless to say, Raag and his Counselor were not invited. Galmutin assumed the Tec warriors from the Togal clan would remain loyal to the King.

Patel of the Tehlon Clan and Agualar of the Faeylan Clan declined to answer Galmutin's call to arms, marking a strong line of division between the Sons of the Law of One, and the Sons of Beliel, made up of the Baal Clan and the Saliene Clan.

Patel and Agualar returned to their villages and rallied their soldiers, expecting a major confrontation on the lower plains of Planar, where Galmutin and Falmot of the Saliene Clan stood ready to lead their armies into glorious battle.

Raag learned of this planned skirmish along with rallying cries for a different leadership. Many of the Tec warriors were distributed about the outskirts of the continental borders. He mobilized the Tec guards of the Citadel and other Tec soldiers available in the area at the time.

The King's army amassed in front of the Citadel. There were thousands within the two armies now facing each other on the plains of Planar. The King's army, a mere hundred strong, standing for the King.

The numbers were badly unbalanced; however, Tec warriors could easily fight off greater numbers with their unmatched fighting skills, thus evening the balance of forces. The King would lead the attack with the Tecs, driving a wedge between the two armies, hoping to quell the uprising, while reducing the severity of losses in the battle.

The Tec warriors charged into the chaos, with several riding Quanah and successfully opened a wedge between the armies as planned. Some of the Baal Clan possessed several self-fabricated Mash-Mak weapons firing into the herd, effectively disabling the Quanah with several bursts of intense rays of fire. The rays sliced into their legs, crippling them quickly. The dismounted Tecs recovered to engage on the ground, fighting hand to hand combat.

Suddenly, more arrows from long bows, shot from the flanks of the Saliene Clan, rained down upon the Tehlon Clan. Raag, attempted to push back on some of the Baal troops nearby, and was struck from behind with an arrow punching straight through his back and into his chest. He fell to his knees. His body vulnerably exposed to the assault of another Baal warrior holding a sword raised for a fatal blow. Fortunately, another arrow shot clean through the Baal warrior's neck, killing him instantly.

Two Tec warriors rushed to the King's side, pulling him out of the fray to withdraw him to the safety of the Citadel and immediate medical attendance.

Before long, the battle subsided with the victors, Galmutin of the Baal tribe standing alongside the remaining survivors of the Saliene tribe screaming the 'King is dead', long live Galmutin, the new King of the Realm.

Raag lay in his bed with bloody wraps partially exposing the arrow still protruding from his chest cavity. The medical assistants wanted to break the head off of the arrow in order to remove the shaft from his body. The tip of the arrow sliced into the right side of his heart. He was bleeding internally.

The technicians declared it was too risky to remove the arrow. Yet, it was not a good outcome either way.

Raag, weakened from the excessive loss of blood, lay motionless and unable to speak. The king's chamber was filled with onlookers, adjutants and Tec warriors waiting to learn of the King's condition. Three medical assistants worked to clean the wound as much as possible, while others prepared elixirs to ease the pain.

By morning of the next day, Raag passed, while many shouted Galmutin's name. Preparations were made to wrap his body in white robes, the body placed into a funeral canoe(an Agar) stuffed with sweet fruits, some meat of the Beshinwar and palms from the popul trees. The canoe was carried down to the inlet sea by Tec warriors, where it was released into the water. A rain of blazing arrows found their way into the boat, now sailing toward the western open sea. It was a fitting funeral pyre for a much-honored King, a warrior's death and a warrior's salute.

Yokar declared to the Court.

"I will not stay within the City of the Realm. I relinquish my position as Counselor to the King Regent."

Then, he gathered many of his personal items, made his way out of the City of the Realm, retreating from the madness that had befallen the kingdom. He was unwilling to abide by the ways of Galmutin and the new Techlogi, while still favoring the old ways more as a recluse.

He sought higher ground, beyond the petty and brutal conditions he knew would follow with Galmutin's reign. His new destination, the slopes of Palinor, a proper sanctuary for a weary Overseer.

On his way, he concluded that he would keep a diary of the Atlantean empire, including much of his temple knowledge and experience.

Perhaps in the future, beyond his vision, there would be hope for a better life. His diary, he thought, *'might help to make for the basis of a new and wiser colony'*.

The armies of Galmutin, the Sons of Beliel, defeated the Sons of the Law of One on the Plains of Planar. They didn't stop at the battle of Planar. Galmutin sought to continue the attack while he possessed an army, on all fronts against all enemies of the Realm beginning with the Lemurians.

The sailing ships and under water machines carried the Mash-Mak weapons to the Lemurian shores. They launched their attack on the Lemurian settlements with awesome fury, burning their dwellings, and incinerating the inhabitants. The Lemurians suffered great losses leaving little to return a single volley of retaliation later.

Galmutin's ascension to the throne would be marked by his return to the original days of Atlantis, when battle became the underpinning of the culture. He wanted his ascension to the throne unquestioned, established because of his aggressive rulership. He proclaimed that trouble in Atlantis was due to the coming of the outworlders. As King, he immediately proclaimed the penalty of death to any outsider that was not a citizen of Atlantis.

Soon, after Raag died, Galmutin ordered the

three Taoi to be reoriented and synchronized in their frequencies. This action left the inhabitants without a power grid. The Yaga Clan(the Builders) could not understand the purpose of this change with the Taoi. Despite their protests, the Taoi were turned and aimed at the skies, the point of departure and home to the outworlders, the Plaeides Star System.

The new regime did not realize the enormous energy and power of the triangulated light beam, was, in fact, inadequate. This ray of fire, would not, could not reach across the vast distance of space between earth and the outworlder's star system. They did not understand that it would take thousands of years for the beam to arrive at its intended target. Days and weeks went by, while they continued to send the beam into space. At the same time, the new King Regent requested the star gazers to keep their viewing scopes trained in that direction to confirm the destruction of the outworlder's home planet.

Meanwhile, many expeditions were carried out using airships with Mash-Mak weapons mounted on board. They ventured to many outposts in

Central and South America, established before by King Raag, to vaporize all inhabitants, leaving only the physical structures and artifacts remaining. Galmutin wanted all remnants of Raag's reign removed from existence, for fear that another rebellion reflecting Raag's philosophy might someday arise.

At this time, Galmutin ignored the warnings the earth presented, that something else was coming. Signs of falling stars(asteroids and debris from space) continued to fall to earth and upon Atlantis, followed by ever increasing land quakes. Their intensity and periods of activity also increased. Buildings began to indicate cracks in the walls and roof structures fell unexpectedly. Some weaker buildings actually collapsed during some of the land quakes. The people cried out to Galmutin to find a solution to the problem.

One day, the gazers noticed a bright and burning object, likened unto a star, approaching through the zone of the constellation of Taurus. In and around this new burning star, whirled many other objects. The burning star also contained behind its path a great long tail. They described this star as a great and terrible Sky Dragon. They named it Bellarius(the nemesis). The gazers came to Galmutin and declared their great concern about this ominous apparition in the sky.

Galmutin scoffed at their claims and believed them to be a bunch of frightened old women. Again, another divergence from Raag's reign, then gazers were considered a significant asset to the Atlantean culture and governance since the arrival of the outworlders.

Each day that passed, the ominous luminary continued to approach the solar orb called the One. The gazers believed at some point perhaps, a great and terrible battle would arise between the Sky Dragon, Bellarius, and the One.

The fishermen came to the gazers proclaiming that the fish of the sea numbering in the thousands, emerged onto the shores of the inlet sea dead without any explanation. The fishermen were frightened by this event. The gazers went to the king and proclaimed this and other strange occurrences too. Cahwyll were seen to fly in strange patterns in the sky just before diving into the earth to their death.

As the ominous luminary got closer, the sky changed and the night altered to make a longer day. Unlike the normal light of the One, the luminary offered an additional strange reddish glow upon the land. More and more objects fell out of the sky in increasing numbers, causing panic in the streets of the Realm and the outlying districts.

The gazers watched in horror as the luminary passed by the One, making the One explode with angry fiery plumes that reached out into space toward the earth. The coronal ejection created a massive shift in the cold magnetic energy of the earth making the river waters move out of their resting places. The waters of the inlet sea moved into the City of the Realm, reaching the outer fortifications of the Citadel.

The polar ice also began to melt rapidly too, due to the proximity of the two stars and the solar flash event from the One. In many areas, the shoreline changed drastically around Atlantis. Remarkably, King Galmutin refused to divert from his purpose, remaining steadfast with his decisions to pursue his enemies around the world and beyond. Meanwhile, he ignored the catastrophic effects the celestial events were causing on the motherland. Every day, the builders (Yaga Clan) worked hard trying to keep up with the ongoing destruction. Taoi beams still converging to fire toward the Pleiades. The skies had darkened with ash. The ash and dust shrouded the solar orb of the One, limiting the strength of the Taoi. The priests controlling the huge crystals, needed to increase the power applied to the beams. So, they adjusted the crystals to vibrate at a higher frequency, a frequency they believed would compensate for the lost light of the One.

The agitation of the high frequency created a resonance within several underground caverns below the continent. Gases of methane trapped inside those deep underground chambers, over hundreds-of-thousands of years, began to heat up expanding into enormous pressures. The pressures excited the caldera of Scartera stimulating greater eruptions of magma and much more ash.

Finally, the methane within the chambers exploded. Different parts of the continent, where chambers were located, suddenly collapsed and those parts sank into the sea. The once great continent of Atlantis, now reduced to five islands.

Galmutin fearing for his life, ordered the remaining scientists and skilled engineers and builders to make ready to board the experimental airships designed to enter into the outer regions of space, their final destination, a final escape plan.

They gathered supplies and equipment and boarded the three airships and set their course for the nearest planet, called Aronak(Mars). The gazers calculated the journey would take longer than expected. Aronak had not quite reached its closest position to the earth.

5 months later, the three ships landed in the area they called Rhodia(Cydonia), between the planet's cratered southern highlands and the smoother northern plains. An ocean of water sprawled out far and away, giving Rhodia a distant beachhead with the possibility of a plentiful water supply.

The atmosphere was breathable but much thinner. The Landing party struggled to unload their supplies and equipment, struggling to breathe, while preparing for their new colony settlement.

Meanwhile, the continuing passage of Bellarius caused the earth's magnetic field to change polarity. In addition, the axis of the earth's poles shifted more than 25 degrees. The tectonic plate holding the five islands of Atlantis moved slightly nearer to the southern regions of the poles. The five islands remained intact while the remnants of the Atlantean civilization struggled to recover from the tumultuous upheavals. With Galmutin gone, along with the other governors, it was necessary to appoint new governors and a new King.

Now it was Demot of the Faeylan Clan, as King. His first order of business, he demanded that a solution be presented to survive the instability of the continent.

The engineers and builders suggested to make giant drilling machines powered by smaller Taoi. They would dig deep into the earth, well below the continent, and perhaps link to other continents by way of their tunneling. After designing the digging machines and creating smaller Taoi to provide the power to drive them. The drilling plan, brought before the new Council, became a much labored argument about the arduous task of drilling holes deep into the earth.

Meanwhile, the new Martian colony of

Atlantean refugees continued to rough out a new living on the strange planet.

The Planet's magnetic field was much lower as was the gravitational force. This greatly inhanced the new resident's agility and strength, which increased their chances for survival. Their food supplies dwindled forcing them to feed on the small lifeforms frequently roaming the area. The water supply they carried with them had also diminished.

The small alien tribe soon made long journeys to discover the ocean, a fresh body of water, that lay several thousand leagues from the settlement. The excursions to retrieve the water needed, would last for many months. Only the strongest were chosen to make the arduous journey. Those journeys would occur only during the warmer seasons.

Life in Atlantis often brutally harsh, prepared the landing party for similarly harsh environment on Aronak. There were no trees within reach of the settlement. The remaining builders fashioned stone huts and pieced them together with the red clay and water as mortar. When survival did not preoccupy their concerns, more ambitious projects began. The builders constructed a 5-sided pyramid as a hollow mound, dedicated to their new god Beliel. The mound served as a new temple sanctuary.

They also wanted to celebrate their survival by erecting a large stone face large enough for Beliel to see, dedicated to their greatness and superior intelligence and the their new god Beliel. Much of the culture of Atlantis was discarded by necessity. There were no enemies on Aronak. There were, however, more objects falling from the skies on Aronak. They were often smaller stones that could easily be avoided by retreating into the pyramidal mound for protection.

Life on Aronak finally seemed to be reasonable. The remaining gazers used their viewing scopes to observe the status of their previous home planet and its subsequent changes with astonishment. All seemed well until a new wrinkle in their survival strategy began to fall apart on Aronak.

The thinner atmosphere and weaker magnetic fields of Aronak did not keep the invisible force of cosmic radiation from penetrating to the surface.

At first, the weaker members of the landing party grew ill. Terrible lesions appeared on their bodies. A painful and agonizing death followed, rampaging through the colony.

Galmutin realized their escape from certain doom on earth was only delayed. After three years on Aronak, all members of the landing party finally died.

After a thousand years passed, a large meteor arrived with a terrible impact. The force of the impact swept away the remaining magnetic field as well as, the thin atmosphere. Soon the waters of Aronak dried up through evaporation.

The once New Atlantean settlement, now over run and consumed by dust storms, leaving the remaining artifacts of the colony mostly buried, removing any signs of their existence on Aronak for all time to come except the face and the 5-sided pyramid. They would never know the actual outcome of the motherland back on earth.

The tunneling machine, in concept, seemed quite simple and easy to produce, however, the task soon became very difficult. Many problems erupted in the midst of the design and construction. These problems seemed to be adversely affecting everyone. The smaller problems, somehow disturbed them and they quarreled. All of the altercations kept delaying the progress of building. The ability of the machine to dig somewhat automatically, to continue indefinitely without pause, was extremely attractive and a high priority.

There were many trials of specific designs. Many tried and many failed to satisfy the requirements of the tool. Each time, the new design presented a weakness that was not anticipated. Failure after failure occurred, as many new designs were tested, more frustration mounted.

Suddenly, a new idea occurred to them. The new idea was so advanced it made previous approaches seem even more inadequate. They built the first prototype and put the machine to the test. The machine exhibited some spontaneous destructive vibrations from time to time, concerning them a little, but it was more efficient than any other design. The new machine was strong. Its actions faster than before and promised to reach the desired depths more quickly. The question remained, will it hold up to the task?

Now, the builders could begin the drilling process with greater confidence. They believed their goals would be met. With their new confidence, they managed to convince the King. Then he declared the drilling to begin.

In the drilling process, a question arose about how deep they should go? One of the priests said prophetically.

'Perhaps it's our destiny to create a bridge between all continents. They would come to the center of the earth, in the joining there, a chance to form a new way, a way that would live within a great city.'

The idea of drilling holes all about the earth seemed, at once preposterous. Yet, as the idea swept across their minds, it developed traction. The idea began to enjoy more support. This idea was new. More than adventurous, possibly dangerous, giving the idea an alluring and tempting quality.

From that point forward, the team of Atlantean engineers/builders launched their way into the earth burrowing a hole deep below the continent. They knew that too deep would subject the crew to extreme heat and too shallow would mean the tunneling might emerge from the surface from time to time. A median point was decided. They would drill only where the temperature did not rise beyond a few neft(degrees).

The tunnel was actually larger than the machine cutting it. The cutting process was really a disk or many disks, rotating. Those disks mounted with many Taoi activated to emit beams that pulverized the stone. The resulting tunnel left behind, a hole many feet larger than the pattern the beams made.

After many months, the tunnel depth reached the ten-mile level. The tunneling machine proceeded to move forward horizontally for many months. After encountering a cluster of huge quartzite deposits, the tunnel collapsed partially burying the digging machine.

One crew member died in the collapse while others managed to escape. The collapse brought down several large pieces of crystal weighing several hundred tons on top of the rotating disk mechanism. The damage to the disk was unrepairable in the tunnel, which meant more serious delays. While having to discard the broken disk, leaving it aside, another disk would need to be constructed, but it could only be constructed above ground.

A small skid attached to the rear of the machine escaped the damage. This allowed part of the crew to ascend to the tunnel entrance after several days of travel. Many more months passed until the surface engineers could assemble another drilling disk. The surface engineers did not have enough of the small Taoi grown to complete the new construction. As the Taoi seeds started to grow, that also demanded more time. A full year passed before the new disk was ready for the descent into the tunnel.

Once the new disk was brought to the collapsed site, further collapses had occurred during the rescue crew's absence. The machine was completely covered and had to be excavated from the tons of rubble. When the rubble was cleared, the new disk finally configured to the machine, they pushed onward for a few hundred leagues without incident, until another obstacle appeared in their path.

The temperature suddenly rose 75 neft(degrees) and drilling had to stop. The crew left the machine to investigate. Placing their hands on the wall before them, revealed the temperature too hot to touch. They could also hear rumblings of sound along with what sounded like the hissing of a dragon. For fear they may have disturbed the home of the 'Earth Dragon', they decided to turn abruptly to the right and drill around the area. The drilling crew were only a few leagues away from a magma flow near the base of the Scartera volcano.

The drilling crew had to stop again. The machine broke into another small chamber full of methane gas. The friction of the drilling disk ignited some of the gas and one crew member was badly burned from the explosion. Now their work went more slowly in order to prevent another explosion. Their progress, impeded once again in that direction, forced them to again dig further downward. They continued in the downward direction for another ten miles until the machine suddenly jolted, the disk spun much faster. A wall of dark green crystal appeared before them. The drill broke suddenly through the dark green crystal and as pieces broke away, the drill emerged on the other side, with the disk spinning wildly without resistance.

The drilling crew exited the drilling machine to see what had happened. After climbing through the narrow gap, between the rotor and the wall, the view ahead presented a wondrous scene. A huge cavern lay before them, many miles high and hundreds-of-miles across, complete with running streams of water, meadows of different grains, a forest of Popul trees and palms spread out across the cavern floor. Many small cavities burrowed into the walls, arranged sporadically along the hillsides, suggesting small domiciles. In the central area, contained many circular structures jutting above all the rest, as towers among a cluster of lower towers.

The engineers looked about and concluded this was a city built by someone else, long since abandoned, but by who, they thought? The crew felt this was a true sign that the gods favored them with a marvelous sanctuary-retreat. They decided their first task was complete. This is the sanctuary they were looking for. All could come to this place, live here in the times of great distress. The decision to go on drilling to other lands from there was delayed. It would be the King's decision, if the tunnel connections from the center they discovered, would or should be continued to other lands.

Two crew members took the skid and ascended to the entrance of the tunnel to tell the King what they found. The King met with the new Council to discuss their evacuation plans. He stood on the veranda of the Citadel of the City of the Realm and gladly proclaimed the blessings of their gods to all the remaining people. They needed to prepare for their evacuation and enter the great tunnel.

Upon hearing the good news, the populace of Atlantis gathered up their belongings. The scientists, priests and engineers gathered up as much of the Techlogi, crystal records containing history and accomplishments, as much as they could carry. The mass exodus of all the remaining clans proceeded to the great tunnel. It took many months of travel through the tunnel before reaching the cavern entrance.

Soon after the majority of the Atlantean populace had arrived, people began to mysteriously disappear in the night. Soon, it was discovered that they were not alone in the new city. The small domiciles were home to large spider-like creatures, entering into the city, attacking and dragged away victims for food.

It was clear, the city was not abandoned, but devastated by the assault of these deadly beasts. Fortifications were quickly built to keep them out, while at the same time, battling the fierce multilegged carnivores. Then, a new discovery of another beast emerged from the other end of the cavern.

It was a mammoth sized centipede. The horror of seeing this creature roaming around the city terrified the new inhabitants. As it crawled along, its many legs pounded against the cavern floor with an ominous multi-tapping sound. The King suffered from total shock. He wondered if the miracle from the gods providing the colony, with a perfect retreat from the chaos above, would now threaten them with extinction below. The invasion of a much larger threat, seemed to complicate their survival. There was no real solution for the spider infestation looming dangerously just beyond their fortifications.

To their utter amazement, the centipede began to hunt down and eat the spiders.
When all of the spiders had been devoured, the immediate danger quickly subsided, worry over what the giant centipede might do filled them with terror. The centipede crawled away, retreating back to the entrance where it emerged. The question remained, did it retreat because it was simply no longer hungry?

They quickly built a stone wall covering the entrance to be sure. After these events past, work to adapt to the city continued. The marvelous attributes would continue to surprise and delight for many years, as the Atlanteans assumed possession of the strange city for themselves.

The King's advanced development continued to evolve until he appeared radiant. His mind expanded to new revelations regarding the welfare of his people in this new underground land. He knew that things had to change.

He began to realize the backward and destructive manner that was the long history of his land above. He wanted to lead the people into a new way of being. He wanted to usher in a world where peaceful living could flourish. He stood on top of the tallest tower to reach out to all the people. The acoustics of the cavern supported his calling, with great amplification. The sound of his voice boomed with only a slight echo to the crowds below.

The King spoke.

"People of Atlantis, by the grace of the One, we have been led to this great sanctuary where we have the opportunity to create a New Atlantis. In honor of this hall below the earth, I proclaim a new way, a way for all our descendants to reap the harvest of our deeds, deeds not based upon violence and death, but great and wonderful deeds that are based upon life and the new life that will support the planet well into the future. For that, I shall give our new city a new name. It shall be called Shambala, a sanctuary for all peace-loving beings. Further, this realm shall be forever more called Shangri-La, the city of everlasting Light of the One.

"Perhaps one day, when all of the chaos is complete on the surface, and the heavens return to their natural order, we shall once again rise to the surface and spread this new way of our culture to the other surface dwellers all around the planet.

***

While the refugees of Atlantis busy themselves with the erection of a new and peaceful culture. Havoc begins again on the surface. As Bellarius swings around the solar orb of the One, its orbital path comes so much closer to earth bringing more catastrophic changes to the planet. The earth shifted its axis by an additional twenty degrees.

The tectonic plates of the remaining continents begin to slide around causing many volcanic reactions all around the planet. The sky darkened and the air suffocated with Sulphur fumes. The island parts of the Atlantean continent sank into the ocean's tidal rampage, leaving only one island left.

The island the Atlanteans called Poseidia, named after the god of water.

Now the island found its final resting place in the southern region of the planet. As the skies remained dark the light of the One remained cloaked for many thousands of years. The atmosphere chilled followed by the coming of the ice forming over the land. Many miles thick, the ice encompassed and stretched beyond the isle of Atlantis. The great ice sheet began to descend to all parts of the land surfaces.

The once great continent of Atlantis was a now a barren wasteland of snow and ice, uninhabitable to any living creature, with temperatures ranging well below150 neft. The glaciers both north and south, crushed over the lands, often with winds exceeding 120 miles per hour. defining the new location of the southern polar region now known as Antarctica.

The entire role of the King changed. He was no longer a king of his people but a spiritual leader. His title also changed. He was now called by the other priests, the High Lama(high teacher). His dwelling became a palace lamasery where the new culture of ascension to the One, became the order and practice of the day.

The High Lama kept mostly away from the people, appearing only at festivals celebrating their devotion and gifts from the One. He spent many hours of the days passing in deep meditation.

The High Lama began to see a new purpose behind this new city and their presence there. He realized that all of their efforts would be to understand the many ways in which Shangri-La could be a future resource for all mankind. It would become a reservoir of vast knowledge and wisdom, prepared and waiting until the rest of humanity was ready to receive the divine gifts from the One.

Many Thousands of years passed and the High Lama realized that due to the special properties of the city, longer life and greater health was possible, befitting the importance of their new task. The city rested on one of the largest deposits of pure gold and the cold magnetic force running through the veins of gold, the rivers flowing over it, developed a strong rejuvenating effect on everyone living there.

The physical stature of the people changed also, no longer brutish musculature, but taller and thinner, with craniums that grew elongated to accommodate greater mental prowess and cognitive function. Their skin became very light in color, devoid of the direct light of the One, could be described as albino. Their eyes and their color, grew darker and larger to adapt to the dimly lit cavern environment. Their hair thinned, becoming lackless in color, more to a whiter shade.

Large worms buried within the floor of the cavern, harvested to become a source of new material for clothing, they called it sulk. The artisans wove the material with inlaid gold and silver offering a beautiful tapestry of garments layered one over the other, in a robe-like fashion.

The pieces of auriculum refugee priests brought along, behaved differently deep inside the earth, compared to their effects and use on the surface.

They studied them carefully and realized that the gold and cold magnetic forces changed their properties giving them a wonderful sensitivity to all kinds of vibrations, in particular, the vibrations of the voice.

Down below, deep in the earth, it was not just the power to amplify the sound of the voice as it was above. These blue crystals became a medium of transformation on the consciousness of the mind, a calmness of the spirit and a dramatic increase in mental focus, offering new possibilities to make them key to a new level of development.

While experimenting with the auriculum, they infused the auriculum at the bottom of forged crystal bowls, whose diameters and depth could create very smooth sounds of singular frequencies and tonal qualities. Many such bowls were created and could be rubbed with cloth saturated with a resin from the oils extracted from the skin of the worms. This resin would grip the sides of the bowls and make them agitated to vibrate their tones easily.

At first, these singing bowls formed a wonderful musical arrangement. Metal bells formed over the bones of the spines of creatures found in the caves, provided another set of sounds that were more like tonal percussion instruments which when played together, complimented the melodies of the bowls.

Ceremonies involving the bowls, bells and chanting of the monks to the special sounds they developed, gave rise to a new set of spiritual patterns which they called Vril Muntrah. These patterns effected all of the elements in different ways. So, the priests began to document those various patterns and catalogued how each pattern would, in turn effect, each of the five elements.

Much study was given to the five elements along with increased clairvoyant observations, they realized the five elements could behave as more. After many hundreds of years of practice and experimentation, 72 different properties of the 5 elements could be assigned, meaning 72 different kinds of water, fire, air, earth and spirit.

As these practices continued to develop, a new reaction emerged in the form of movement. A slow kind of dance developed to accompany the musical forms they played. Then within the movement, they realized that certain body movements seemed to resonate with certain sounds. Their study continued to understand the movements and what they meant.

The monks analyzed how the sounds resonated in the body and formed a pattern of movements that would effect the endocrine glands and nervous system to effect the quantum of time and space around the body. The first effect was upon the air element. With uttering certain sounds, and certain body movements the body would loose its weight and begin to levitate. The priest/monks explored applying this principle to other objects like large stones. They realized that combinations of sounds played on their instruments accompanied by chanting of the Vril Muntrah on the stone, the stone also could be levitated. The size and weight of the stone object was irrelevant.

The builders realized that this deeper understanding allowed them the possibility to build large structures on the surface, when they were ready to return.

Another aspect of these sounds occurred when applied to stone. By varying the sounds and applying these sounds to the stone offered a different effect. The stone surface vibrated very quickly and became soft and almost plasma-like. When two stones were in close proximity, they would fuse together. Now the two stones became as one stone.

The sound-movements applied to their bodies effected the space as well as, the time. They realized more than one dimension existed within the same space and same time. This activity became another element of training. Priests could move their consciousness forward and backward through time allowing them to predict what reality would look like in the future and re-examine what the past presented.

This presented a new possibility to examine their past mistakes and offered solutions for the future. They could learn from their mistakes, apply what they learned and then test out their insights while viewing their future. The view of their future seemed to be highly localized. They did not have a sense of what was happening on the surface.

The question of the conditions on the surface became a heated debate. Many were satisfied to remain below in a world undisturbed by the wrath of nature and the unpredictable events from the sky that might again place them in danger. Others differed strongly arguing that access to the surface should be of paramount importance. Even the underground environment could be unpredictable as well.

The decision to make a large opening in the earth, which could provide access to the surface, for those who wished to exit the underground, in times when exploring the surface conditions would be beneficial.

They applied their new sound Techlogi and began a slow boring of a great hole at the polar region. The location of the hole was considered carefully and deemed important. They felt too much material vaporized from one surface area alone, could cause the earth to wobble on its axis. They didn't want to create another tumultuous chaotic response resulting in more catastrophic consequences. They felt to disturb the balance of forces with the rotation of the earth by removing large amount of mass along the periphery was unwise.

It took more than 200 years to complete the polar opening. Their airships could now exit the underground city and allow them to explore the surface easily. When the first explorations occurred, they were shocked to see vast sheets of ice covering most of the earth's surface. They searched far and wide, but no evidence of their original home world was found. Worse yet, no life appeared to exist anywhere in their searches.

They returned to the city beneath to report their findings to the High Lama. There was a meeting of the elders to discuss what they would do. It was decided that drilling holes to the other continents from below was their only choice.

Thousands of years past while the other tunnels were completed. During that process, they determined that another hole could be created at the other pole, which would ensure the balance of rotational forces could be maintained while at the same time complete access to the underworld from both poles could be possible.

Signs of the great ice sheets retreating offered hope that life on the surface could be restored and the exposure to the One could once again be enjoyed by the under dwellers.

***

Several other extraterrestrial craft from the Lyra star system landed in a region near the area now known as the upper African plains. Even though other large areas of land mass were still covered by ice, this area seemed warm, balmy and fertile, giving the Lyrans an opportunity to think positively of colonization.

The Lyrans were tall and bipedal, but their head and facial features having a distinctly strong feline appearance. They set about creating an entrance to their new city to honor the arrival of their supreme leader. First, they erected a large replica of their supreme ancestral leader lying prone facing the eastern rise of the sun. They called this the Sphinx, named after their ancestral leader.

Their plan also, to create a long row of sphinxes leading up to the large prone cat at the front of the avenue. No sooner had they began to create the structure when the earth suddenly tilted on its axis some few degrees causing wide spread atmospheric storms and the water from the nearby sea, overwhelmed their building site and burried the large Sphinx in sea water.

A quick decision concluded by the landing party, that this planet was not suitable for colonization due to the high probability of unpredictable cataclysmic conditions. The Lyrans left, leaving behind all building artifacts, still in place. They never returned.

Several hundred years later, another craft arrived from the Mica star system. A reptilian species known as the Arcturians came in a ship designed for exploration and surveying. They stayed long enough to determine the planet was rich in many minerals, including gold, silver and certain exotic metals useful to their technological needs. This trip did not include reserving a landing party that would stay behind. They left after their mining aspirations were satisfied and planned a return trip with many of their engineers and soldiers to secure their mining operations later.

As the tectonic plates continued to move around and crash into each other, areas that were buried deep into the earth were exposed, but surrounded by large mountains souring into the sky by miles. These became the mountains of Tibet. Parts of the original city of Shangri-La were now exposed to the light of the One, but still shrouded by mountains of snow and ice. A small portion of the underground city, though exposed to the surface, remained separated and secluded from the outside world. Descendants of the original Atlantean colony now populated the surface part of the city and kept the original name of Shangri-La.

The remaining parts of Shangri-La still within the earth, took on a different name later called Agartha.

The great tunnels that connected the five continents, emerged in South America, Asia and Eurasia and North America as well as Africa. All entrances to these tunnels were kept secret and only known by descendant remnant priests to this day.

Actually, underneath the mountain called Shasta in the North American continent still has some of the Atlantean drilling equipment sitting within the tunnel for thousands of years, that led to Agartha.   Another mountain in Peru, South

America, called Huascaran Sur, also has digging apparatus as well as, remnants of Taoi stones left in that tunnel.

Many times, the orbit of Ballarius, (Nemesis the One's twin star) passed the One without incident. This time, one of the larger planets in its solar system, Nibiru, (the Sumerian given name was earth crosser) came very close to earth. The people who lived on Nibiru came to earth and landed in the area of the Tigris and Euphrates rivers in the land of Mesopotamia.

Mesopotamia is an ancient region known in the modern-day as Iraq and parts of Kuwait, Syria, Turkey and Iran. Part of the Fertile Crescent and viewed by modern day archeologists as, the cradle of civilization. Mesopotamia was home to the earliest known human civilization on record, known as the Sumerians of Sumer. Their primary city was called Ur. Until recently discovered, Ur was considered to be a mythological city, as was Troy until found, many years before.

When these Nibirians landed, they arrived in a star cruiser called an Ehdan. The leader of these extraterrestrials was a king, called Anu. His people were Anunnaki. (the Sumerians used this name, to mean ('those from heaven came down').

They were very intelligent reptilians, tall, with

green eyes having slits as pupils. Their scales were a dark green in color. Their hands bore only four fingers with sharp claw-like nails. There were a little over 300 crew members; including scientists, doctors, and engineers, as well as, the King, his two sons and daughter, Enlil, Enki and Isis. They had surveyed the earth from space, then determined the was planet rich with many minerals. The one mineral they wanted was gold, as much of it as they could find, and earth had plenty.

Nibiru enjoyed a sophisticated culture with very advanced technology, but after many millennia, a small problem soon became a serious problem arising on their planet. Their magnetic field decreased in strength, depleting much of the atmosphere, due to solar winds sweeping it away, not unlike Mars. The Anunnaki engineers knew it was leaking off slowly. Eventually, bringing certain doom if they could not stop the leak. In the short term, they needed to seed their atmosphere with white powder gold, a derivative of pure gold, manufactured after being processed by their laboratories on board their ship. The white powder gold could bind some of the atmospheric molecules together and keep the atmosphere from blowing away.

Many of the crew, called Iggigi, were brought along to work as miners. At the first scan from space, the gold content seemed to be present within the two rivers. The engineer/miners began to filter the water of the two rivers for the precious mineral. After many months, it was clear, the amount of gold fell short of the quantity needed.

They sent out scout ships to scan the areas within a 5,000-mile area. To their delight, many rich deposits found within the earth, were discovered in the nearby deserts of Egypt, Chad, Niger and the Congo. Now they would have to dig into the soil and rock for the mineral.

They immediately brought 200 workers, and the drilling equipment by way of shuttle transport to dig the new mines. Small villages were created to provide shelter, while they worked night and day. Soon the Iggigi returned to Ehdan, their colony ship, and complained to the King.

"This mining work was far too difficult for them. They wanted help and refused to continue until they got assistance.

In the meantime, the engineers and scientists interacted with the local inhabitants of the city of Ur. The people of Sumer thought the sky people were gods coming down to care for their people. They offered celestial knowledge, knowledge of agriculture and metallurgy as well as, health sciences and even improved their communication skills which included a writing system. The language formed into organized cuneiforms and applied to clay tablets. Hundreds of years later, many thousands of clay tablets were completed and stored in special ziggurats(pyramids) for their historical libraries along with the knowledge acquired from the gods.

The problem facing the king and the future of their planet, depended on real and immediate solutions. Enki and his sister Isis suggested to the king, after conducting their surveys of the region, a possible solution.

"Father, Isis and I have noted many bipedal creatures roaming the land. Isis suggested a genetically modified creature could be developed from those existing lower lifeforms. They were not very intelligent, compared to the people of Sumer, but they were strong and could make an ideal work force after they were altered.

Through the sampling of the blood of these captured creatures (Neanderthals), Isis and Enki tried to contour their DNA to build a new lifeform. After several trials experimenting with these dumb animals, they found them to be too regressed to be of any use in sufficient time. They needed to find another bipedal lifeform that exhibited greater evolutionary development.

Again, the scout ships returned to the deserts to look for similar species that might serve their purposes. Eventually, they found another species, also bipedal which responded to their approach with less hostility and more curiosity. These were the Cro-Magnons, one higher step on the primate evolutionary chain. They rounded up many of these creatures and brought them back to Ehdan to be altered genetically. They needed them to be smart enough to operate their machinery, smart enough to learn some of the Anunnaki language and follow orders obediently, but not smart enough to rebel against the Anunnaki.

After several hundred years, about 150 modified hybrid Cro-Magnon creatures emerged with a more upright stature, much less hair and a larger cranium containing a new fore brain capable of simple reasoning. They fed and clothed them, and protected them from the environment. In exchange, these new hybrid miners worked hard night and day, supplying the Anunnaki with copious amounts of gold bullion, which in turn, they processed into the white powder needed for the atmosphere. The powder then shipped to Nibiru in supply ships by way of Mars, a closer planet functioning as a storage depot, closest to their planet's position.

Once again, the altered throwbacks were cast off later, exiled to the northern wilderness in a place called Nod. They continued to procreate and developing a relationship with the other large colony of hybrids called the Anem people, (the Atlantean outcasts).

Enki differed with his brother Enlil about the homo-Sapien-Sapiens he and Isis created. Enlil hated them and could not stand to be around their brutish nature. When they were finished mining, he wanted to destroy all of these abominations Enki created.

Enki secretly admired his new creations and wanted to give them a fair chance to evolve. So, he secretly added his reptilian blue blood (blue in color because of the high copper content) to the DNA mix offering the hybrids a new quality of self-awareness and greater curiosity.

The time had come when the King determined that the mining operations could stop. He planned to return to Nibiru before it passed the perihelion of its orbit around the One. He ordered his two sons and daughter to return with him to their home world.

Enlil said King Anu.

"Father… these Homo-Sapien-Sapien beasts should be destroyed before we leave. They may procreate and over run the planet. When we return, we will have to deal with that problem."

The King replied.

"Enlil, you are wise to consider this. So, let it be done."

Enki wanted desperately to save his creations. He arranged for most to escape before Enlil could exterminate them. Enki led them out of the Ehdan and guided them to their hybrid counterparts far away, in the Land of Nod.

When Enlil found out about Enki's treachery, upon Enki's return, a battle ensued between them wherein Enki, in a fit of rage, killed his brother Enlil. The incident was brought before the king and he ordered Enki to leave Ehdan, exiled to the land of Nod with his created clan.

Isis pleaded with the King.

"Father…you can't be serious to leave your son, my only other brother here on this forsaken world. It's cruel!"

The King replied.

"Do not worry about your brother, he can take care of himself, I'm sure. Besides I want him to stay and consider the impact of his decisions. Do not worry daughter, he will have the comfort in knowing I have installed Regional Governors to rule in our absence."

Meanwhile, King Anu left earth with Isis, leaving Enki to fare for himself in the wilderness.

The King felt the land needed supervising until his return. He assigned three of his generals to rule over the wilderness regions; Jehova, Vishnu and Ahla.

Enki didn't mind his exile, spending much of the next 3600 years continuing to teach those of the Abra and Sapien throwback people. Later, he returned to the city of Ur where he continued to teach the Sumerians more about celestial mechanics and about the Anunnaki, their home world Nibiru and their culture. The empire of Sumer eventually collapsed. A new civilization emerged in Mesopotamia called Babylonia.

The hybrid Anem mated with the hybrid Homo-Sapien-Sapiens. Their offspring were beautiful to behold, unlike the reptilians, their eyes were large and oval, their skin fair without scales and their hair retreated to cover only their scalp with long blond strands. They continued to develop intellectually, and created their own language.

The Fallen spirits of the nether world of Aldeberan, looked down upon these female hybrids with awe and wonderment, and very desirous of physical contact.

They came to earth and seduced the hybrid

females with their guile. They made them mate with them. Their offspring came along with some surprising changes in their DNA. Their growth factor, greatly enhanced, making them giants standing from 12 to 25 feet in height.

For many hundreds of years, the giants(called Nephilim) roamed many regions assisting with arduous building tasks. Their voracious appetites consumed enormous amounts of food supplied by the Abra people. When the food supplies became scarce, the Nephilim became angry. They attacked the Anem people and devoured many of them. From that time forward, their taste for blood ended with their eating of their own kind, as cannibals.

Another cycle of Bellarius came, Nibiru passed closed to Mars, where a scout ship was sent to earth to find and retrieve Enki. The King wanted to see what Enki had accomplished in his absence. The King was pleased about the progress of the hybrids, but shocked about the giant creatures.

The King told the engineers.

"This world has become infested with giant monsters. The earth needs to be cleansed of this aberrant and dangerous species."

The engineers on Nibiru set about to generate a strong magnetic impulse toward another of Nibiru's moons, Malia, close by Nibiru's orbit, making it swing very close to the earth. The resultant close pass caused violent earthquakes and tidal waves to sweep across the earth in a great deluge, killing off almost all humanoid species, including the giants.

Only a few exceptions were saved. Again secretly, Enki's interference worked to preserve some of his special creations. He warned the hybrids of the planned flood that was to come. He taught them how to build an ark that would save them. He provided the survivors with several vials of animal embryos.

Enki returned with the King back to Nibiru knowing he had saved the new hybrids from destruction. Enki provided a new way of survival for the earth. He agreed with his father, the giants created by the fallen, along with his creations had to be removed. Of course, he purposefully left out his plan for their survival. The only way to provide a chance for the new homo-sapien-sapiens to exist and flourish would be if they completed the ark in time. Gilgemesh, the leader of the hybrids enlisted the giants to help build the ark quickly. The great flood ravaged the land before the giants could board the ark.

The Anunnaki left the earth and returned to Mars. They brought back the white powder gold and distributed it into their atmosphere. However, the efforts to save their civilization failed ultimately. The atmosphere eventually evaporated anyway, leaving Nibiru a dying planet. The Anunnaki would have to evacuate and find another star system to colonize.

A planet, in the Reticulum system, with its star Epsilon Reticula became their new home, but their settlements were troubled by interference from the existing grays, from Zeta 1 and Zeta 2, the binary sequence stars. The grays were very aggressive and many conflicts finally ended in several wars lasting for a thousands of years. Atomics were used and as some retreated back to Mars, the grays unleased several atomics there as well. The Anunnaki would never return to earth.

***

The Arcturians, also a reptilian race from the Draco system, decided to investigate further with their earlier surveys of planet earth and its neighboring planets. Their planetary system illuminated by a dark red giant, provided little heat or light to their system, making them extremely light sensitive. Since earth was illuminated by a yellow bright star, posed a significant problem with the idea of a permanent colony.

Though the atmosphere on earth was suitable, the surface of the planet, covered by large bodies of water, kept them from approaching. Meanwhile, they explored Mars, Venus and Jupiter for possible new outposts in the interim, waiting for the waters to recede on earth, their precious future prize.

They found the conditions on Venus and Jupiter to be too volatile to make settlements feasible. Mars would become their second choice, as it was a short jump to earth for their large Cambrian cruisers. The atmosphere on Mars was almost negligent. The temperatures were nominal for reptiles, on the cooler side, and the sun's light dim enough that they could remain on the surface for long periods. They built settlements both above and below the surface.

Finally, thousands of years had passed. The Arcturian armada arrived on the planet earth's surface. The ice sheets had retreated on earth exposing large continents of land which allowed access to their need for gold, used not for anything other than bartering on other worlds. Some of their ship designs possessed large scale systems for extracting the metal by infrared beams heating the crust and then sucking the metal into large vats aboard their mining ships.

The Arcturians originated in the Draco star system. There were many reptilian species that populated the galaxy, but the Dracos and their culture are one of the oldest in the galaxy, going back at least a million years. They are exceedingly intelligent and cunning. Their prominence existed primarily because of their innate aggressive and violent nature. Warriors all, living within a hive mentality.

The organic-evolutionary trait of these creatures is built upon a very militaristic behavior. Reptilian in appearance, covered head to toe with dark green scales, claw-like fingers totaling 6 on each hand. The eyes yellow in color with cat-like slits for pupils. They were built large in stature with prominent musculature, usually more than 9 feet in height. Unlike other reptilian species, their snout was elongated and their mouths filled with many rows of sharp teeth, resembling a crocodile on earth later. The males or worker/warriors dominated the society, while the few females marked by those who possessed wings, could fly.

There were others, who also possessed smaller wings but they remained more or less ornamental and could not fly. Interestingly, the females were the leaders/and queens, revered as supremely important to the entire colony of hives. All warrior/workers were sworn to protect the queens of their respective hives.

They have been star voyagers for hundreds of thousands of years, traveling in very large Gambrian star cruisers, more than 2 miles in length, capable of faster than light travel. Though Dracos experimented with time travel, later on, those experiments continued to be unsuccessful and often with tragic results. That aspect of technology, considered not only dangerous, but an unwise activity to pursue.

Over time, the Dracos spread out and advanced the exploration of other solar systems, raiding planets of their resources, capturing other species as slaves to their empire. The hundreds of Gambrian starships became a virtual armada, containing thousands of warriors and particle beam weaponry heretofore unmatched anywhere in the galaxy.

Many species feared their presence, much in the same way that the Roman army was feared by peasants later on in earth's history.

Their knowledge of astrophysics and elemental physics combined to place them far above most species. Their exploitation of other worlds revealed rich sources of iridium and thorium deposits, which later became the heart of their fusion drives and warp capability.

In the Mica system, they operated many mining colonies and created a variation of a Dyson sphere (an array of luminance receptors built to wrap around a star and pull the fusion energy away in the form of a plasma, from around three of the suns in the system. Immense transcoders transported the plasma beams to other planets and stored the energy into gigantic fuel cells, on planets around those solar systems. This action provided almost unlimited power to the many colonies of the local systems. This development, led to their plasma sourced fusion drives and the particle beam weapons mounted aboard the Gambrian cruisers, which other species could not compare or defend against.

The warriors wore an individual 'skirt jacket', a kind of tunic, over their breast and upper legs, which was powered by a fusion belt wrapped around their waste, to function as an exo-skeleton of invisible armor (a force field), impervious to any weapons they might encounter. In short, they were almost invincible soldiers.

The flood waters receded exposing many lands. The population of the earth was minimal on the surface and the Atlantean remnant had no plan to emerge onto the surface.

When the Gambrian cruisers arrived and parked their ships in geosynchronous orbit around the planet, they scanned the surface and did not find any significant life forms that might present resistance to their landing and claiming the planet as their own. The general rule in the galaxy: all planets essentially uninhabited by sentient beings became fair game for mining rights. Though no one in the galaxy would stand up to the Arcturians if they decided to invade and take over a colony on an unregistered planet in any of the known systems.

Unlike the Anunnaki, the Arcturian geological surveys concerned themselves with land deposits only. Much of the primary interest in the minerals present was the gold. The other deposits of irridum, thorium and uranium represented only trace amounts, these were minor and of minor interest, but the gold content of the planet was large. Plans to extract it were already underway by the crews of the lead ship, preparing to disembark with several smaller craft loaded with their highly specialized mining equipment, capable of heating and melting the metal and pulling the liquid into vats for ultimate molding into ingots or plates made easy to store and transport back to the mother craft.

Other craft designed for further exploration and surveying landed from the other mother ships and immediately began to scan the other land masses for minerals and any creatures suitable for their needs as slaves and workers on their home world Draconis Prime, or in the mining colonies in the Mica system comprising several hundred planets.

Other cruisers also surrounded the planet Mars and Venus for possible mining interests. Mars did not provide any useful materials other than Iron and Palladium, both which had been discarded in favor of their newer alloys which were both lighter in weight and denser molecular structure needed for Gambrian cruiser hull manufacture.

Structures housed hundreds of military troops set up in circular rows around proposed mining sites, defending against any forces that might oppose their presence. This planet would be easy and free of conflict.

Many of the gold veins meandered deep into the crust of the earth's outer mantel. Their sophisticated heating apparatus would not function on deeper levels. Sporadic volcanic activity also caused many delays. The commander of the first mining ship communicated with the supreme commander aboard the Gambrian lead ship.

Commander Zod spoke.

"Supreme commander Durrk…I am reporting on the progress of our first mining operations. The larger veins of the mineral gold seem to vary in density close to the surface, but improve with depth. Our mineral exchangers will not reach such deep penetrations. I am requesting that a contingent of troops begin a tunneling effort to reach these deeper levels. It will become tedious and perhaps much slower. But the rewards will be greater."

Supreme Commander Durrk replied.

"Commander Zod…Yes… I have received reports from the other mining ships with similar problems. The unexpected volatility of the volcanic activity on this planet leaves some serious questions as to the viability of this resource. The other commanders have also suggested similar approaches to deeper mining. Yes… I authorize the use of troops in your case too, to engage with tunneling.

"Any signs of intelligent life in your area?" The supreme commander continued.

Commander Zod replied.

"No sir…nothing to report…some lower life forms roaming around but they steer clear of our operations for the most part."

Durrk added.

"I am getting some dire messages from one of the mining colonies in the Mica system. It seems there is trouble brewing on some of the planets. The Regional Overseer reports large groups protesting, and in some cases, violence has broken out. I will need to get back to you later.

Durrk out."

Meanwhile, on Ganamede 4, the fourth planet around the sequence star Regulus in the Mica system, many the miners rebelled. They managed to break into one of the security stations controlling the electronic collar transmissions, releasing several hundred slaves from their neck collars.

The mining camp descended into chaos, now under a major siege of the facility. Some of the miners managed to capture several pulse rifles and hand explosives stored in the ordinance bunkers. Subsequently, several of the Arcturian guard were killed, while at the same time, the rebels threaten to extend their violent assault onto the other mining camps as well. Then new reports of other planets in the Regulus solar system, initiated communications with the rebels on Ganamede 4 and vow support in their impending revolt with their own mining camps as well. This news became very disturbing to the supreme commander.

Commander Durrk immediately recalled all of the troops on the surface of the earth. The commanders of the individual mining operations, declared that an immediate evacuation to the mother ships would be impossible. First, the mining equipment would have to be put back onto the landing craft. Then there was the problem of the gold.

The individual commanders complained and didn't know what to do. Durrk then communicated to Zod to rally all of the mining commanders in one location so he could relay the circumstances to all at once.

All of the reptilian miners and warriors deployed underground had no idea what was happening on the surface. The urgency of the situation prevented relaying the news and the supreme commander did not want to delay their departure for the Mica system any longer than absolutely necessary.

Several lieutenants were left on the ground to keep the mining operations running until the motherships could return and gather their gold remaining on the ground. In a matter of hours, all five of the Gambrian cruisers were reorganized and positioned to make the jump to faster than light speed as soon as the supreme commander ordered it. It would take several days to reach the mining colonies in the Mica system. Durrk now anxious to get back and quell the uprising before matters became worse.

In the following days, some of the reptilian miners emerged to the surface expecting to be greeted by their superiors and found no one around. The landing craft were gone. Many questioned why they left without letting them know. While several attempts were made to reach the landing craft and the motherships on their personal communicators. Their short-range communicators could not bridge the vast spacial distances already achieved by the Gambrian cruisers.

The lieutenants knew very little of what had happened and could not explain to the miners and soldiers why everyone left in such a hurry. They told them the motherships would return eventually, and they should go on mining the ore until they returned.

Weeks turned into months then years passed. Even the lieutenants were hard pressed to give a reasonable explanation about the absence of their comrades in arms.

As mining life carried on, food and water supplies became limited and rationing began. It was clear the much-needed supplies would not be available in the near future. So, mining operations ceased in favor of hunting the local game for food and then the search for fresh water became very important as well.

One night, the lieutenants gathered all of the soldiers and miners together to discuss their options. The sun's brightness precluded that they could not remain on the surface. So, enlarging the tunnels for their habitats seemed prudent. Much discussion centered around their long-term existence on this strange planet. Some difficult decisions had to be made, considering they were on their own.

Finally, the lieutenants made their proclamations.

"You all know the situation we are in; our leaders have abandoned us and we are definitely on our own. The other leaders among us here, have decided that we should take matters unto our own and take possession of this planet for ourselves.

"Further, we feel that we worked hard to gather the mineral gold and it belongs to us now, not the empire. The earth planet is ours now. We don't have ships to escape so let this place be our new home.

"We will burrow deep inside. Perhaps, we'll find larger spaces deep within the planet, where we can live beyond the sun's light and flourish and multiply our numbers."

The miners and other soldiers agreed to each take his share of the mineral gold, and keep it for themselves, disavowing their allegiance to the empire.

As it turned out, the Gambrian ships never returned even until this day. The refugee reptilians remain hidden deep within the earth's crust as a separate civilization hidden away, hoping that someday, they too will be able to live on the planet as surface dwellers. From time to time they abduct humans for DNA augmentation for their needs, hoping the hybrids can eventually live on the surface.

The Atlantean continent, that dominated the Atlantic waters for hundreds-of-thousands of years, went through enormous upheavals with serious geological formation changes.

Near the top of Mt. Palinor, two shear rock faces thrust high above the clouds. Like two giant pentacles, they appeared to stretch beyond their strength and balance to endure any test of time. At some earlier point in time, the two rock faces began to lean and pitch toward each other forming a kind of apex or arch. It is at this place where the arch formed, where Yokar's cave existed.

Due to the nature of the arch formation, the entrance to the cave was well hidden, ensuring Yokar's continued privacy and solace in his voluntary retreat from public life.

Life in the cave had settled into a highly regimented regime of exercise, meditation and introspection. From time to time, he would leave the cave for the slopes below, gathering vegetation and killing a few darwon(a rabbit-like creature) for his supply of food for a month. In the winter time, passage from his cave to the lower slopes was cut off. He planned ahead for those times when he needed to store more food.

Yokar had disavowed Techlogi Just before he left the City of the Realm in protest. After many heated altercations with the New King and the new members of the Council, he pronounced openly, he wanted nothing to do with these violations of natural law.

"This way… he commented… distorts the way of the law of One. It destroys our principles and thus destroys the utter foundation of our inner strength and honor."

Once he settled into cave life, he reminisced about his former life before he became a Priest, Overseer and ultimately Regent Counselor to the King.

It was a time well before the arrival of the outworlders. At the time, the King had three consorts within the court. Two of the consorts were discovered to be barren, but the third bore him a son, the future Regent Prince Raag, who would ultimately become his Heir and King.

When Yokar was 1200 cycles of the passing of the One in age. He was old enough to begin his fight training that all male citizens had to undergo. He began with entering into the military under the tutelage of an expert Tec warrior called Zoku, learning all the fighting skills Tec warriors would possess, wielding a sword, long lance, the long bow and hand to hand combat as well as, dealing with the manner of devious ways that Lemurians create mental deceptions and hallucinations.

His skills increased in time, to perfection. He quickly moved up through the ranks of foot soldier, and as lieutenant, commanded a garrison of Tec warriors. After leading several successful skirmishes with the Lemurians, he rose to the rank of General of the Realm.

After 300 more cycles of the One, Yokar wanted to understand and embrace the laws of Nature and the ways of the stars. He entered into the Temple of Knowledge devoted to the God Ishtar and the One Most High. As a Neophyte, he became familiar with medicinal herbs and the making of elixirs and concoctions for healing. Then, he was introduced to the Teylon Clan (overseers), an offshoot of the Tasher clan (gazers). He was taught how to view the sky and the arrangement of the stars, the constellations and their use in choosing conception times.

He learned about the Natural laws, including the ways of the Earth Dragon and Sky Dragon and all their pathways embracing the Earth. Yokar learned about the three basic laws of the universe; the positive light force (Agogik), the negative or shadow force (Magogik) and the Neutralizing force (Peruitii Rogalin) and how they influenced all manner of activities in daily life. Eventually, after mastering this knowledge, he was ordained as a candidate for priesthood.

All candidates are put through a series of tests, if successful, these tests would mean becoming fully ordained as a priest of the temple. He was fortunate to have received tutelage from the Law Givers, Kantsu and Tiantsu before their passing, at the age of 3250 cycles of the One.

These tests would determine strength, fortitude and mental acuity. To stand on a tightrope stretched between two stone pillars 50 leagues apart as the rope dangled in a long slope. This made keeping balance while not moving, incredibly difficult without falling to the ground.

He had to climb the long stairs along the rim of Mt. Sepula, three times. One climb counted 2300 steps. This had to be done within a specific period of time which meant almost running the whole way.

He had to hold up a length of tree limb (1.5 leagues in length) from a Popul tree, with a 100-pound stone dangling at one end for two hours, without letting the stone touch the ground, one for each arm.

Then he was given several tests at choosing the right color stone, from a batch of different colored stones, matching each stone to the priest who placed each one of the stones on the table. Once chosen, he would take each particular stone to each priest.

In addition to this psychometry, he was given images telepathically of places where he needed to go, finding specific objects to return to the priesthood. Afterward, when he successfully found all of the objects and had selected the correct stones, the priesthood would create a sling containing the objects and precious gems representing the same color of stones he correctly chose during the test. Later upon ordination, the sling would be presented to him to wear over his garments indicating his rank and authority.

Upon ordination, his hair would be shaven completely down to one lock, worn on the left side and clasped with a golden band. (similar to the Egyptian pharoahs in Ramses'time) The band represented a symbol of his wedding to the priesthood, bound to his hair that holds his entire history held within the DNA of his hair.

After 150 cycles of the One, Yokar rose to the status of Overseer/Counselor and served as fair witness to the High Council of Governors.

While functioning as General to the Tec warriors, he mated with three concubines afforded to him by his rank from the Togal Clan. A son and a daughter were conceived by way of the Tasher clan. He visited the hatchery several times to observe his offspring. Once they were 100 cycles of the One old, he stopped coming and relinquished any parental concerns by law.

Life on the continent was reasonably peaceful with the exception that from time to time, a Trok (Tyrannosaurus Rex) would break through the outer barriers in the upper foothills of Palinor and Scartera and feed on the inhabitants.

Many thousands of nights were spent in the cave doing temple practices, such as, the Taumlec Arc. This practice, designed to resolve the problem of time perception that would ultimately lead the practitioner to engaging with the shadow kingdom of heaven. It comprised of using two sets of Jub Jub beads that would give an accurate accounting or the passage of how much time would be spent on the four directions, starting at the groin, then to the right shoulder, then to the crown of the head and finally to the left shoulder, each direction governed by 4 colors, blue, red, white and green respectively.

In addition, Vril(the subtle language of the Gods), was silently spoken at each direction with the un-named organ (Atlantean-UTRJGHYPTKA) located at the base of the throat. 4 groups with a series of letter combinations, where each letter is given a phonetical vowel combination. So, the first Vril was ONJNG, followed by RETRUSHII, AUMRET, KPTHAN corresponding to the 4 directions. This was done continuously for 30 arcs

(1 arc is a round of the 4 directions) which would require about 18 hours of time.

Yokar also practiced the Dragon's Breath, a complex pattern of movements involving smacking the back of the head after standing in one place, taking several deep breaths followed by a complete exhalation until a vacuum was created in the solar plexus. The vacuum would be held for 5 minutes until the energy rose within the groin taking the form of a coiled viper looking similar to a corkscrew shape.

4 postures were assumed in a given round. In each posture, a combination of calling up the earth dragon and bringing down the sky dragon with these movements would meet at the vacuum place of the solar plexus. The first 4 postures would make one round at about 1 hour. Then the second level would be 4 times the first round, or 4 rounds comprising 16 postures at 4 hours. Then the third level would be 32 postures at 8 hours continuing until 9 levels were achieved to complete the practice. This invigorated and empowered the life force including all three forces in combinations leading to a singularity or unification to the One

Most High.

When these practices were continued in the
temple until success was achieved, a staff would be
made of Kinar wood, (similar to the original
walnut species of tree) hollowed out and filled
with Auriculum to the precise length of the
practitioner's spine and topped with a Taoi crystal.
This 'Staff' became known as a 'wand' many
hundreds-of-thousands of years later, used in
Druidic and Wiccan practices in Eastern Europe
and Gall (France).

Also, Yokar would practice something called the
Torax, an inner alchemical meditation involving
the mental construct of 3-sided pyramids filled
with the energy of sexual force, revolving around a
vertically positioned 4-sided pyramid with the
3-sided pyramid apexes pointing toward the 4
corners of the 4-sided pyramid base.

This structure would turn clockwise, while at
the same time another set(4) of 3- sided pyramids
filled with various negative emotions pointed at
the 4 corners of an inverted pyramid. The two
4-sided pyramid apexes are facing each other. This
inverted pyramid would rotate counter to the upper

pyramid. When the energies of each are drawn into the 4-sided pyramids, the two are merged together to form a dodecahedron at the heart Puuka. This meditation would then be repeated at the throat Puuka and the crown Puuka sequentially. This practice resolved the three knots of the heart; Fear, Pride, and Greed. Believed to be the cornerstone of Atlantean spiritual transformation.

The last practice Yokar performed was something called Skrying. An isosceles triangle, gold in color, imagined in the mind with a red Orb on the right corner and a green Orb at the left corner. The head was tilted slightly so as to hear the heartbeat from the carotid artery pulsing next to the inner ear canal, then flashing the two lights on and off alternately at the rhythm of the heartbeat. In time, the consciousness is cast into the triangle and moving to the left would give a view into the past and moving to the right would offer a view of the future.

In time, Yokar reconsidered his judgement cast down on his brothers and lamented. He could not judge them without also judging himself. He realized he needed to forgive himself for his fascination with Techlogi and its seduction.

Soon, he turned his judgements into compassion for all their ignorance and pride. He also knew he could do nothing against the groundswell of rage to conquer in that ravaged land, with a lust for power and for power's sake.

After many years of seasons, he realized there was little above the tree line that could provide heat and light. So, he brought a few small devices from below, to provide heat and light within the cave in times of need. Later, he would even bring a portable Slater-ring (a magnetic platform on which a series of metallic-crystal rings are placed on edge, twisted to rotate quickly) to record his diary entries.

Once the rings began to turn, they could either play back any stored information to a viewer or, they could be made to record sounds and visuals of events in real time.

Yokar feared for the possible loss of knowledge in the temples and the scientific knowledge acquired, recorded by the gazers about the stars and their movements. He wanted to record his knowledge of science and the spiritual work onto the rings for posterity, a kind of personal spiritual diary of his meditations and experiments.

Yokar had no real interest in the history of Atlantis, other than as an allegory or moral message, that could transcend time for all future generations to come, functioning as a compass for all righteous behavior.

His grief was not for himself but for his people. They lost their way, falling out of balance with the Natural Forces they came to understand, the gods then returned with a fury and brought down most, if not all, aspects of progress the people worked so hard to achieve.

Yokar said.

"I freely admit, I too was seduced by the clever means and ways of Techlogi. It worked its way into my mind by offering a promise of release from toil and hardship, a truthful part of the underpinning of the nation that was once Atlantis.

"It's a terrible thing to see something awful happening, and there is nothing you can do to stop it!"

With all of the turmoil occurring below, the memory of Yokar had faded from physical view and re-entered the minds of people more as a legendary mythos. After so long, the legend became the tradition of a hero, kept alive by the storytelling of Yokar's exploits; first as a Warrior, his spiritual accomplishments within the Temple of Apollon, and finally his negotiation skills as a Statesman and Overseer to the Realm's King.

Galmutin, as King, did not recognize Yokar as a hero, in fact, just the opposite; more as a criminal and as a seditionist and coward too, as a traitor to his people. Even his spiritual skills of healing and clairvoyance were twisted by Galmutin into dark and sinister forces from an evil sorcerer. He needed to be careful. He could not be recognized.

In truth, time provided the perfect cloaking of his identity to anyone in the valley. His fear went unrealized. He found he could move around through any public place without anyone recognizing him, only that he was a stranger visiting in the village.

Yokar added to his diary.

'Before the second cataclysm came upon us, I was told that a messenger from Lemuria was making the climb to meet with me. I thought this was strange. My heart felt a deeper urge to withhold my resentment of the Lemurian treachery. When the Lemurian arrived, I was shocked to see him so fragile and pale. I greeted him friendly. I enquired as to who he was and why he came to me?'

The Lemurian said.

"I am Shetah, I am a scribe of the great Lemurian leader Bushitri(a Cephalopod) of the Skiiffig clan."

Then I asked.

"Are you ill? ...You do not look well, Lemurian.

Shetah answered.

"My health is of no concern…only that, which I brought here for safekeeping."

"Great and Noble Overseer, we of the Lemurian Tribe, know well of you. I have come to you for help. Our world is coming to an end. It has been prophesied. So, I have been commissioned to bring to you our most sacred relic; the Ngualaa, a ruby cylinder incrusted with the seal of the High Leader and contains all of our history, our celestial knowledge and our spiritual insights."

Then, as I turned my back for a moment, the

Lemurian disappeared into the mist of the mountains, leaving behind the ruby cylinder wrapped in the skin of a cahwyll .

'Opening the cahwyll wrapping revealed the beautiful cylinder made up of hundreds of ruby plates tied together through a central hole which penetrated all of the plates stacked together. I marveled at the deep red color shimmering in the beams of cave light. I folded the wrappings over the cylinder carefully. Then laid it on a shelf near the cave's entrance.

Yokar wondered about the outworlder called Adalon. He would often look upward, peering into the night sky looking for the Orion system. Following to the right, he could see the family of stars Adalon called the Sisters of Pon, their final destination. Perhaps one day, he would go deeply into the quantum, and in his meditation, find Adalon lounging comfortably within his dwelling and telling stories of the strange people of earth to his offlings.

He stood at the mouth of his cave, on evenings when the shadow of Scartera shrouded the light of the One, allowing him to peek through the clouds at the valley far below. As he pondered the possibility of his being the only Atlantean left, far and away, he suddenly saw the collision of Raika with a smaller moon and the debris falling toward the earth in the evening sky.

'Many of the parts of Raika entered the earth's atmosphere, bringing a rain of fireballs upon the great western sea, then it happened.

A very large fragment entered the atmosphere looming ominously over the continent of Gwandana. Upon impact, a great and terrible shaking and a thunderous clap exploded upon the continent with a cracking sound and the rush of furious wind rolled out and away from the impact and flattened everything in its path.

I cried to think of the horror of all those Lemurian souls crushed by the crashing moon. As a mountain of water rose up out of a quiet surface of seawater, I witnessed before my weary eyes, the supreme final act of the gods… the utter destruction of Lemuria, gone for all time, as it began to sink into a lake of fire all around its edges, plunging deep below the surface.

The cave was way above the chaos and disaster,

but my view of the massive destruction wiping to extinction an entire race from the face of the earth was both breathtaking and horrifying…Then I wondered if the rest of Atlantis was next.

Consequently, I spent the next 1500 cycles of the One devoting my consciousness to serve the One Most High and her laws.

After that, my body began to glow and a great and terrible shaking started within my body. I knew my time had come. As my awareness exploded, I looked around fondly at my humble dwelling, with all of my furnishings and diary that I would leave behind.

My body dissolved into dust leaving nothing behind to prove my existence.

All in the cave would eventually turn to dust as well, save for the crystal rings of my diary and the ruby cylinder of Lemuria, both artifacts reflecting a golden age that will be forever forgotten, buried for all time to come. Then, later perhaps, emerging as the fanciful imaginings of a future child.'

It is interesting to note, Atlantis is still considered mythology by mainstream archeologists as well as, Shangri-La. Shangri-La was made public by the book, 'Lost Horizon' by John Milton. Though there is some interest to prove where Atlantis might have been located, in the case of Shangri-La, it is considered strictly poetic fantasy. No efforts have made to locate that place. Of course, according to the author, its location was somewhere in the Tibetan mountains. Because the location is within the borders of China, no outsiders would be allowed to investigate.

The two fabled civilizations are either now underground/ or below miles of ice in the case of Antarctica, or perhaps above ground, but buried inside mountainous regions of snow and ice, essentially inaccessible, which is true in both cases.

Though it cannot be confirmed, the remnant of the lost island Atlantis is truly now resting under millions of tons of ice in Antarctica. In very recent times, the United States has declared Antarctica off limits to anyone that does not have a top-secret clearance. That stirs up curiosity, whereas, before, many Nations have had scientific installations on the southern continent for decades, until now.

It seems clear perhaps, the US has discovered something in the way of important artifacts or even remnants of a lost civilization there. The government is preventing anyone from seeing it, or even knowing about it. This smacks of the same 'national security' issues around the fabled Area 51, in Nevada.

Tracking the migration of Atlantean refugees as they dug deep into the earth to escape certain doom from catastrophes in the past, in addition to, the many rumors from local residents about these tunnels interconnecting continents, in places like South America and Mt. Shasta in Northern California, suggest these tunnels may in fact, exist.

It is purported, only a select number of people, considered as ancient initiates, have the knowledge of their whereabouts, in those locations. One such Tibetan monk by the name of Losang Rampa referred to an opening where digging machines from Atlantis still exist. Again, access is all but impossible.

It is the author's belief that the existence of Shangri-la, as a modernized version of the Atlantean culture, metamorphosed into a peaceful and loving colony after hundreds of millennia, is a secret colony devoted to the preservation of ancient knowledge for the future of mankind. They live a very long time and prepare for a time in the future, when the masses of the world cease their madness and self-destructive tendencies. Then, these monks of Shangri-La might offer the knowledge to the masses to make use of this knowledge and flourish.

At the same time, there are many legends of the 'little people', such as, the Leprechauns of Ireland, and the chachalacas of Finland. All of these legends fall into the general abyss of fantasy and imagination.

Perhaps these underworld creatures venture to the surface through these unknown tunnels to get a glimpse of the surface dwellers. The author believes that some of these stories reflect a bit of truth. The descriptions given by eyewitnesses, of these creatures possessing 'devil' like appearances; having scales for skin, green or yellow eyes with slits like reptiles, are in fact the offspring of the original remnants of the Arcturian contingent, left behind many hundreds of thousands of years ago. They only appear at night, as one Saami Indian told the author in Finland, referring to his father's stories, who purportedly, actually saw and spoke to them on many occasions.

Abductions, are described in personal human accounts, of reptilian beings, experimenting on abductees in their deep underground facilities, for the purpose of creating reptilian-human hybrids.

This would allow the remnants to escape the underworld of their ancestors, to walk on the surface, as the surface dwellers do in the light of the sun. One such US military base, in Nevada is called Dulce. The base, mostly underground, is purportedly operated jointly by the US military and Aliens. A secret contract to provide the US with advanced technology in exchange for subjects for these top-secret activities by the Aliens is also conjectured.

The fact that more than 2,416,365 people have disappeared in the US from 2017-2020, is disturbing. When, according to the Hadley-Ward

Statista Research Department, report from 1990-2021 indicate shocking numbers. On average, missing persons from 663,621 in 1990 to 980,712 in 1996 have never been found with only 4,400 unidentified bodies found during that period. This is a staggering fact, considering this has happened in a modern period of time, where the forensics of the most sophisticated technologies are available for surveillance and investigation.

Perhaps, in the next few years, more discoveries will be made and full disclosure will actually occur, as our government authorities reveal more of the truth.

For tens of decades the religious outcry that 'God created the heavens and earth' to include only humans on earth, now seems preposterous in light of the fact, there are hundreds of millions of galaxies with trillions of stars in each. Now with our new special telescopes, revealing each of those stars having many planets. It is estimated conservatively, that hundreds of thousands of those planets are earthlike and probably have advanced civilizations living on them. To say that we are not alone, that we have never been alone, is ipso facto confirmed.

The argument that there cannot have been visitations by extraterrestrials because it is impossible for any species to be able to cross those vast distances of space. Thousands-of-light years apart, traveling at 10% of speed of light, would not allow even the closest star systems, eleven light years away to be reachable in a human lifetime.

For humans, traveling faster than light is impossible according to Einstein. But there are some holes in the relativity theory. It does not include the more modern theories of quantum mechanics and space-time concepts.

This does not mean that another highly advanced culture, perhaps a million years ahead, living in another star system many hundreds or thousands of light years away, have not solved the faster-than-light problem.

The author believes Einstein-Rosen bridges(wormholes) exist already in deep space constructed by Alien technology. They are used regularly by many advanced races, which allow easy crossing of vast distances between solar systems and even between galaxies.

The story of a lost civilization on earth, existing many millennia before now, and assisted by Aliens from far away, is plausible. Some 6,000-year-old Sumerian tablets actually describe such visitations in their historical records. Many other cultures around the world represent such visitations in petroglyphs on stones and inside of caves. These indigenous cultures have legends that tell about these 'sky people' coming down to greet them. So, it could also be readily realized this assistance by Aliens may still be continuing even now. They were involved, according to these ancient accounts, in altering the DNA of early humans like Neanderthals, or Cro-Magnons into Homo-Sapiens-Sapiens, a true evolutionary leap in development.

Scientists have not found the missing link between Simian primates and humans on the 'normal' evolutionary scale. That suggests that the normal evolutionary process on earth had been altered. Perhaps the Aliens may have desired to provide a boost to life on earth, speeding along its higher development. That would explain why they keep coming back, abducting people to check on our progress or some plan for hybridization.